'We woke up'

Lynfree J.

DEDICATION

This book of Short Stories is dedicated to everyone who was once asleep yet made a conscious decision to wake up.

CONTENTS

ACKNOWLEDGMENTS

I am forever grateful to every person who has poured into my life.
I am thankful for every heartbreak and failure as it pushed me to
learn the art of transforming my lessons into blessings.

We Woke Up.

December 2019 was a month of anticipation. Unbeknownst to anyone 2020 would come in and wake everyone up from a sleep that many did not comprehend existed.

The pandemic came in and caused doubt and fear. How is it that in the year 2020 America could be unprepared in a way that it would cost the lives of women, men, and children. The pandemic gave a new meaning to 'wash your hands' and 'keep your distance'. Worries of a shut down, thoughts of state borders closing, and the unnecessary rush to purchase toilet paper all were daily thoughts in the lives of people across America.

The Start to the Awakening

Unfortunately, the pandemic wasn't what totally woke the world up. Instead, it allowed everyone to be at home sitting in front of a television while events of the world unfolded before the eyes of all. But why? Why did a few events spark a national outrage? How was racism ignited in a land that is free, a land where people are due a day in court.

What people failed to realize is that one event didn't cause the events of what transpired over months to unveil, instead it reminded Americans of what has been occurring for too long.

But how did people see this now? It happened in previous years, where was the cry? It happened in previous cities yet there were no riots. Why now, why in 2020? Why in the midst of a pandemic is the world deciding to finally wake up?

The Reason Why

Prior to the start of the awakening all concerts were canceled; no waiting in long lines to see entertainers. Airport lines were the shortest it has ever been. People were not traveling because of uncertainty of where Covid-19 may be found. Sports were at a halt. Fans were unable to secure a seat in many stadiums; the entire sports world stood still. Live television shows were finding ways to regroup and provide broadcasting from the comforts of their own home. Jobs were laying off hard workers and dining out was limited to take-out. The world stood still. The world was at home frustrated and confused about what each day would bring. And in the midst of uncertainty, in a time when millions lost their employment, a time when schools were closed, when husbands were home with their wives, children eating dinner with their families, a time when each person was sitting in their living room waiting for directives from a pandemic; time stood still and events unfolded.

How could the world ignore this? The answer is simple; we couldn't. The entire world had no choice but to bring the events to the table and tackle it once and for all.

WE WOKE UP

We Woke Up

We Woke Up

Can You Handle the Truth?

We Woke Up

Happy New Year

"Hurry up, why is it taking so long to grab the blanket? My goodness you are going to miss everything." Lisa shouts. "I'm coming." Yells DJ as he runs out of the house with a large wool blanket. "I can't believe it; the time has finally come."

At once the countdown on the outside television begins. *'5, 4 3, 2, 1, HAPPY NEW YEAR.'*

DJ grabs Lisa and plants a huge wet kiss on her forehead. "The year we have awaited is finally here. May this year be the start of the most amazing year we have ever seen. I love you." DJ then takes his rusted red and black sports hat off his head and places it on Lisa's significantly smaller head slightly coving her long wavy hair.

Lisa embraces DJ and the two hug and kiss passionately under the stars. They discuss their hopes and dreams then without warning, Lisa whispers in DJ's ear. "I have a secret." DJ tries to pry it out of Lisa, but she insists they wait until morning. The two talk and snuggle until they both fall asleep in one another's arms.

Within minutes there are gunshots heard! The couple wakes up abruptly.

"It must be the neighbors bringing in the new year, but to be safe let's just go ahead inside babe." DJ says as he grabs Lisa's hand with urgency.

The two barely walk inside their home when additional gunshots are fired, this time closer than the ones before. Within seconds another gunshot is heard, followed by another. DJ who is putting away the blanket returns to the living room where Lisa was searching the television guide for a movie and, "Oh no." DJ shouts. Lisa is laying on the ground face down; she has been shot.

DJ rummages around to find his phone; he dials 911. He is instructed on how to perform CPR from the operator while waiting for the police and paramedics to arrive. Lisa is not breathing. DJ screams. *"HELP ME, HELP ME PLEASE SOMEBODY, ANYBODY PLEASE HELP ME."*

DJ holds Lisa in his arms, he begins having flashbacks of when the two first met. Lisa was wearing this God-awful orange sweater with a pair of blue jean shorts that looked like it came straight from the thrift store. DJ actually walked up to her and cracked jokes about her wardrobe and the rest was history. The two were inseparable. They talked on the phone for hours each night, went on dates all the time, and after only ten months of dating they found a nice small home located in a quiet neighborhood in the country. They couldn't be happier when in the company of one another.

Sitting on the floor waiting for the police to arrive seemed like forever. Finally, there is a knock on the door. DJ yells for them to enter but the door is locked. He gently places Lisa's head on the floor and rushes to let in help.

As the paramedics tend to Lisa the police ask DJ questions. DJ isn't much help as he doesn't know who was shooting nor did he go out in the front yard after the shooting to get any details. He completes a police report and within minutes Lisa is rushed to the nearest emergency room. The next few hours will be crucial.

DJ is too nervous to drive to the hospital and wait, so instead he calls Lisa's mom and informs her of what happened. Her mom is angered more at DJ than the situation, blaming DJ for allowing her only child to get shot! DJ is too emotionally distraught to argue. He ends the call and starts canvassing the neighborhood. Surely someone must have seen something. He knocks at the neighbor's door but there is no answer. He literally knocks on every house in the neighborhood with very little luck. Within an hour he receives a call from his boss. "DJ, it's Trent, look man I know it's the new year and you aren't scheduled to work today but I need you man, I really need you to come in. We just signed in a huge shipment at the warehouse and it needs to go out ASAP." Before DJ could tell him about Lisa, his boss says, "DJ this is the break you have been waiting for, if you show the higher bosses that you came in under short notice it will look good and you will be a shoe in for the open position. I need you man, see you in a few minutes." His boss hangs up.

DJ tries calling Lisa's mom to see if she made it to the hospital but there is no answer. He makes a snap decision to go to work and keep busy believing that Lisa will pull through. He works a ten-hour shift. He doesn't take a break or lunch, instead he puts all his hurt and anger into working. Soon as he clocks out, he leaves work and drives straight to the hospital.

Upon arriving DJ finds out that Lisa is in room 435. He goes to her room only to find police officers near her door. Not shocked due to the nature of her stay DJ doesn't think anything of it, that is until he tries to enter her room and is stopped!

"Sir, identification please." Says an officer.

"Oh, yea of course, I'm her boyfriend. Here is my ID."
DJ says in a rush.

The two officers at the door look at one another.

"Sir," says an officer, "I need you to turn around, you
have the right to remain silent, you have the right to
an," DJ interrupts in disbelief. "*WHAT*? Um what are
you talking about, that is *my girlfriend*, I called you,
you can ask the 911 operator for the tape, my girlfriend
was shot and I called for help, and I, well, how is she?
What is going on? Is her mom inside? Let me in. I need
to see Lisa."

DJ proceeds to attempt to push his way through the
door but is unsuccessful. The police officers pin him
down and he is handcuffed. DJ is now talking very
loudly and with a strong tone as he is confused.

At once Lisa's mother walks out of the room. She sees
DJ on the ground, now in handcuffs. She looks directly
at the police officers and says, "That's him, that is the
man that shot my daughter. *I DEMAND* justice
immediately!!!"

DJ is hauled off by the police and placed in police

custody. He is utterly shocked and appalled by what has transpired. Lisa's mother never really accepted him and always said her daughter was 'too good' for him. According to Lisa her mother was only being over protective and met no harm, but now DJ isn't so sure.

DJ is booked as a suspect in the shooting of his girlfriend. He is confident she will pull through to be able to sort everything out. DJ is allowed one phone call. He contacts his older brother. Within 24 hours he is bailed out of jail.

DJ tries everything to get in contact with Lisa. He calls her cell phone, contacts the hospital, and even has his brother drive by the hospital as a 'concerned' friend but he is unsuccessful.

DJ returns to the home he shares with Lisa. Her blood is still on the floor. He breaks down crying. His entire life has changed in hours. DJ is distraught. He cries himself to sleep. Within a few hours there is a knock at the door; it's the police.

Once verifying his identify a police officer firmly says, "We have a warrant for your arrest."

Confused, DJ wants information on why the police is at his home but before he can ask questions the officer informs DJ he is being arrested for the murder of Lisa.

She didn't make it; Lisa is dead.

DJ falls to the floor, he is inconsolable. The police officer pulls him up, handcuffs him, and proceeds to haul him off to jail.

DJ was not allowed a phone call, he has not eaten or spoken to anyone since arrested. He is trying to piece together the events but can't get past the fact that Lisa is gone.

After two days in jail, barely drinking anything other than water, DJ has a visitor. It is a public assigned defender; Raymond.

Raymond introduces himself to DJ and informs him of his options. "I have great news for you DJ, can I call you DJ? I was told that is the name you go by."

DJ shakes his head in agreement.

"Well," smirks the public defender, "I have some amazing news."

DJ, for the first time in days looks bright eyed at the defender in anticipation of what is to be said.

"They offered you a plea deal, a very good plea deal might I add." Raymond informs DJ with a wide smile.

DJ is just staring at his public defender. A million thoughts are now running in his head. He can't even control them long enough to speak. DJ is confused. How is he being offered a plea deal for a crime he never committed. His girlfriend was shot possibly by a stray bullet on the early morning of New Year's Day. Why is he being held in jail? Why is he taking the fall for a crime he never committed? What is going on!

"DJ, my man, hello did you hear me? You were offered a deal. You have never had so much as a traffic ticket on file and being this is your first offense you can walk free in ten years." Raymond then proceeds to take papers from his briefcase. He pulls an ink pen from his jacket pocket. "Simply sign here and it's all over; no court, no media, no worries."

"I need to make a call." DJ says softly.

"Excuse me." Raymond says now looking somewhat muddled. "I offer you the deal of a lifetime and you need to make a call?! Look DJ I will be frank with you, I don't know how long I can keep this deal on the table. It's a good deal. You took a life. Ten years is the best I can do."

"I didn't kill anyone, I never killed Lisa. I love Lisa, I would never hurt her. I don't know how I even got accused of such a horrific crime." DJ's hands are sweating as he speaks. "We were bringing in the new year. We were laughing. We went inside the house we share when I walked away to save a blanket. She hated when I left blankets in the living area. I heard a gunshot, returned and there she was just lying down helplessly. I called 911, then later her mom. I never killed Lisa I don't even own a gun what is going on? Why am I here? How am I getting charged? This makes no sense. Where is my brother? I-I this can't be real, what is going on?"

Raymond pulls a file from his briefcase. "The papers in this file are from Lisa's mother. She said that you called her and confessed to shooting her daughter. You then told her you have 'work' to do and you hung up the phone. She rushed to the hospital. You, over ten hours later, arrived at the hospital trying to 'visit' Lisa. Look DJ she is trying to work with you. You took the life of her daughter yet she was willing to work with the attorney's office to get you a plea deal."

Raymond places the file on the table then grabs DJ's arm and states, "Take the deal." He then slides the plea deal papers near DJ, placing the ink pen as close to DJ as possible, looked him in the eyes and firmly says, "Let's end this now; sign the papers."

DJ is now trying to fight tears. "This isn't right, I need to speak to Lisa's mom. I need to remind her of our phone call, I didn't kill Lisa. I didn't do this."

Raymond begins pacing back and forth in the tiny room. "DJ, I have kids. I actually have 4 children to be exact and I would lay down my life for them. I would never want to imagine my life without them. You took away a mother's child. You took a life. A parent never forgets something so tragic. That phone call will stay with a parent for life. Now I don't know the details of the call because I wasn't on the call but a mother was, a mother who will never see her child again, a mother who will never be able to watch her child get married, have babies, or do simple things like go shopping and visit over dinner. You took a life and you want to talk to the mother? For what? To have her re-live that night? DJ you seem like a bright young man and we all know mistakes happen. Maybe Lisa was threatening to leave you or she caught you cheating on her. Look I don't know why you did what it is that you did but it's apparent that *you* killed this woman. We have canvassed the neighborhood. There were no random shots heard by neighbors, only the few shots that were fired from your residence. No strange cars witnessed in the neighborhood, no witness of anyone 'riding' or 'walking' near your home; no one. Now again I won't question your motives, but I will tell you this, a mother lost her child because of you and all she wants is justice. If I was her, well let's just say, I wouldn't be so liement on you. Now sign the damn papers!"

There is silence. It is so quiet you can hear a pin drop.

After a few moments, (which seems like a lifetime) DJ speaks.

"I graduated high school at the top of my class. I later went to college on an academic scholarship and worked hard to graduate. I was the first in my family to earn a college degree. I know I come from a small family and we didn't have much money so it may not seem like much to some but it met the world to my family. My brother, who has always been my best friend is older than me, enrolled in college after seeing me graduate. He said I motivated him. One of the nicest things anyone has ever told me, it met so much to me since our dad was never around. Imagine me, the little brother influencing the big brother, definitely happier times. After college I started dating but the women, I liked, well they didn't really like me, then I met Lisa.

She was beautiful, but I will admit that she wasn't my type at first. Yet we talked and it was as though we had known each other for a lifetime. We were different yet alike. Our dreams and goals measured perfectly. We both wanted to get married under a big oak tree with only our immediate family and close friends. We talked about family and marriage plenty. I loved her and she loved me. It was simple. Our relationship worked. We decided to move in together. I still remember her telling her mom, who was so pissed and disappointed when she found out. But we moved in together anyway. A nice little house in the country. It was perfect, we were perfect. I would never hurt her, *NEVER*. She was my queen. The woman I one day wanted to bare my children." DJ pauses. "Lisa should not have died. I should have let her put away the blanket then she may be alive and I would be the one resting and she would be able to live her life. I did not kill Lisa, nor did I confess to killing her; I loved her then and I still love her now."

DJ lowers his head as a tear falls slowly down his face. He is extremely emotional.

Raymond takes a deep breath. "Tell you what, I will see what I can do. I can't make you any promises, but I will see if Lisa's mother can be questioned again just to be sure all of the details are correct. Give me a few days; I will be back soon."

Raymond leaves. DJ spends the next week in isolation. He doesn't want to eat or socialize with anyone. He was allowed to contact his brother, but due to limited finances his family couldn't afford legal counsel. DJ is patiently waiting for the truth to come out. Someone somewhere must know the truth.

Time passes. One day when DJ is asleep in his cell a guard alerts him that he has a visitor. He is escorted to a private room for a visit; it is Raymond.

"Sorry it took so long. I was able to get Lisa's mom requestioned but her story remains the same. She is certain that you confessed to killing her daughter. In fact, against my better judgement she requested to see you. I brought her here, but don't get your hopes up. She made it clear she is not recanting; she wants closure, and well, under the circumstances it's understandable. I will give you both a few minutes alone, per her request. I will be right outside! Do not pressure her she has been through enough! This is merely a courtesy visit!"

Raymond walks out and within seconds he returns with Lisa's mother, Karen.

Karen enters the room and Raymond exits.

Before DJ has a chance to talk, Karen speaks.

"DJ, DJ, DJ, I remember when Lisa told me about you, she said mom he is so amazing, he has a college degree, a good job, and he is such a good man. Lisa always spoke highly of you. Even when the two of you would have little petty arguments, she'd say, 'I'm fine, he works my nerves because he loves me,' she really did love you. Because of her I had to accept you; but it didn't mean I had to like you. Look DJ, I would have never suspected that my daughter could fall for a man like you, yet she did. She fell hard. So hard that no matter how much I fought against it she never stopped loving you. Why? Well, I will never know nor do I care to. I remember the first time I met you she said 'mom be nice' and I was, that is until you stepped foot in my home. Why you? What made her bypass all of the single men to say that's the man I want? I questioned her but she would always say 'mom don't start, I love him and he loves me,' so I would step back and let it go; momentarily. That is until December 30th, when she called me, she was so happy. She said mom you will never believe it, I thought oh no, please God don't let her be getting married, I mean it's one thing to live together but God forbid the two of you marry. Within seconds she said, 'I'm going to facetime you.' I answered the facetime and she was looking beautiful, glowing even. In excitement she blurted, 'I'm pregnant.' My jaw dropped. My heart sank. I was speechless. She said she had just found out that she was 6 weeks pregnant, that you didn't know, as she said she wanted to wait until the two of you awoke on the morning of 2020 to tell you the news. I just listened to her as she spoke about her unborn child, a child she said would be, 'the joy and light' of her life. A child she wanted to name after her grandmother if a girl and your brother if a boy. She talked for over ten minutes; she was so happy yet so naïve. To think that she would be able to have *YOUR* baby and all would be well was propositus. God knows I love my daughter but she was so naïve to real life at times. What kind of life would that child have with the two of you? I knew that I couldn't talk to her as she was on cloud nine. I knew that the only thing that I could do was convince her to have an abortion. We hung up and I gave her ample time to come down from her excitement. I called her early on December 31st, told her happy New Year's Eve then asked if she had told you. She stated no as her plan was still to wait until the two of you awoke on New Year's Day. I asked if she had told anyone, she said only she and I knew, but soon as she told you she would tell the world as she was extremely happy to be carrying 'DJ's baby.' My stomach turned at the sound of that. I then, without thinking it through told her she needed to have an abortion and I would take care of the cost and make all arrangements. There was silence on the phone then she hung up. Can you believe that she hung up on me, her mother?! I called her back but there was no answer. A few minutes later I attempted calling yet again no answer. Shortly after she called me. She said mom you listen, 'I am having this baby, my baby, a baby that I will love and DJ will adore and if you can't handle that then you don't have to be part of our lives. I love DJ and together we are going to be great parents. I know you think I am young and a bit naïve but I have DJ and as long as I have him helping me, then the baby, he and I will be just fine.' She then hung up the phone without allowing me to get a word in.

After that call I sat and millions of emotions ran through my mind. What would the country club members think? What would the neighbors say? Oh, the stares and blank look we will get. How will I explain that my daughter had a, no no no, she can't have the baby! I made up in my mind that this baby could not be born. It was my job as Lisa's mother to protect her. My job to make decisions that would help her in the future.

I knew that she would never have an abortion with you in her life, but without you she may consider it, as she would not be able to raise that baby alone.

I remember her telling me that the two of you would be home together on New Year's Eve and I knew I had to act. Once she would have informed you of the baby it would be too late. I made a few calls. You would be surprised at how easy it was once I explained you two being in a relationship. It was too easy.

You always wore that God awful red and black sports hat; that's all he needed to know.

All 'he' had to do was show up to your house and peep through the large bay window on the one night of the year when shooting guns were not alarming. New Year's Eve, a night when people are popping fireworks, shooting guns, and minding their own business.

"*YOU* were supposed to die that night." Yells Karen with a disgusted look as tears stream down her ruby-red cheeks.

Karen walks close to DJ, spits on him then walks away and proceeds to knock on the door to be let out of the room; she then exits.

Raymond enters shortly after with the plea deal and ink pen. He places it on the table DJ is sitting at. "You have two minutes to sign this document or the deal is off and you will stand trial and I promise you '*we*' will ensure that you rot in a jail cell for the remainder of your natural born life."

Raymond exists the room.

DJ, who has not said a word since Karen first entered the room lets out a loud unsettling roar.

DJ grabs the ink pen, clutches it in his hands, and signs the plea deal.

He now has to spend ten years in a maximum state petitionary for a crime he never committed.

DJ returns to his cell and journals his thoughts….

Love is Blind. When I met you, I fell in love with your soul. Not once did I question the color of your skin, difference in your eyes or complexion of your beauty. I only saw a person, a soul that needed to be loved and I knew that as long as we both consented, were on the same page in this thing called life, then it mattered not what anyone said. You were mine when I saw you, I was yours from the start, never in a million years would I imagine that this cruel world would tear us apart. The sun is now setting you are no longer here and I have the rest of my life to cry heartbroken tears. Our race should not matter, why do they care? Whatever the reason I want to question but because of my skin tone I do not dare.

We Woke Up

All Aboard

"By the power vested in me by God and this fine state, I now pronounce you husband and wife. Sir, you may salute your bride."

The happy couple, Gregory and Gina, engage in a long passionate jaw-dropping kiss in front of over two-hundred guests. The couple, who have been together for several years have become one. They finish their first kiss as man and wife then Gregory surprisingly picks up his bride and carries her away. The couple sneak off to a bridal room and make out. Guests begin to make their way to the reception area. It is beautiful. Lights dimmed, fresh live flowers in every corner of the room, a bottle of champagne on each table, and waiters waiting to cater to each guest.

The happy couple later return to their wedding reception and enjoy a night of dancing, laughing, and drinking with a room of their closet family and friends.

By 2am the party is over and the two are fast asleep in their bed. Within hours Gina awakes in a cold sweat, coughing, and her body in pain. She attempts to stand to walk to the restroom but is too weak. She reaches over to her new husband only to find he is cold as ice.

Gina pats her hand around for her cell phone to call 911 as she is ill and she is quite sure her husband is as well. Emergency responders arrive within twenty minutes. The couple is transported to a local emergency room. They are both diagnosed with the flu and sent home. Instead of a seven day honeymoon the couple spends the next week in bed taking medication.

Gina is up and moving freely around in a week's time but Gregory isn't so lucky. His body is not responding well to the medication and the diagnosed flu is not going away.

Gina, who has been alienated from everyone calls her mom. Her mom answers but is sick as well therefore the conversation ends rather swiftly.

Gina decides to brighten her day by opening some of her wedding gifts. She opens one from her uncle, a griddle, she smirks as her uncle knows she does not cook so this will not be of value to her. She then finds an envelope. She is excited as she believes it is cash inside. Gina opens it only to find it is a letter from her ex-boyfriend.

'Gina, I heard of your upcoming wedding. I am happy for you I really am but I miss you. I went to your wedding to stop it (thought I would have the nerves) but

when I saw everyone, I became nervous. You looked exquisite; I have never seen anyone so lovely. If only you had been mine. You were supposed to be the one that I married. My phone number is on the back of this letter; use it when you want. I will always be here; waiting.'

Gina is sitting in shock; she hasn't heard from her ex in years. I mean they did have a long-term relationship and there were happy times but he was a control freak and to think that he could just come back, then on her wedding, the thought is just crazy to her.

Gina opens a few more gifts, nothing out of the ordinary. She received a towel set from her cousin, gift card to her favorite spa from her college friend, several kitchen appliances, and a robe set. There were a few gifts that Gina did not open as she wanted to wait to share the moment with her new husband.

Gina calls a few of her family and friends to say thank you for the wedding gifts. Out of eight phone calls six of the people were sick; all of who were guests at her wedding. She begins to wonder if something was in the food that may have caused sickness but she doesn't want to ponder on that theory.

A few weeks has passed by. Gina and Gregory have

fully recovered. They decide to go on a five-day cruise since they never had a chance to honeymoon right after their wedding.

The day arrives and Gina and her husband rush to the cruise port. They barely make it on time as Gregory somehow misplaced his boarding pass and it took almost an hour to locate it. Nevertheless, the two aboard the cruise ship.

Almost immediately after boarding Gina ran into 'Brenda' an old friend from high school who was on a girl's trip with three other women. The two ladies, Brenda and Gina spoke. Gina complimented Brenda on sporting the new limited pink handbag with the gray straps that literally just came out a week ago then shortly after the ladies went on their separate ways; they never were close friends, just classmates from the same town.

The first few days on the ship were amazing. Nights overlooking the ocean, alone time away from everyone, no social media or TVs, just a few days of rest and relaxation.

By day four Gina was ready to return back to a sense of 'normalcy.' She loved the time away but four days at sea was enough for her. For some reason she always imagined more people on a cruise and more interaction but this cruise was different, I mean the captain said it was a full cruise but you could count the people and each day seemed like less and less people were around.

The following morning of the scheduled return home from the cruise was nice and quiet; no bad weather, the food on the cruise ship was amazing and the alcoholic beverages tasted great.

As the boat neared the dock a large sound came over the ship's intercom: *'We are not clear to return; we will circle the pier for a few hours and then return. Thank you for your patience.'*

"That's odd," says Gina.

"Does seem odd," states Gregory, "But I've never been on a cruise before and neither have you, it could be basic standard. No different than a plane not being able to land because the crew isn't ready for them or they don't have the landing strip ready. I'm sure all is well; no worries."

A few hours turn to a full day and the cruise ship still has not docked, in fact the ship is now more centered in the water and extremely far from the last dock.

"Babe," says Gina. "I think something is wrong, I mean I am not a 'cruisologist' but um, why are we going further in the water and why are we still on board it's been almost 24 hours, what's going on? This doesn't feel normal to me, does it to you?"

Gregory decides that he and his wife should go and talk directly to a crewman on the ship just to get clarity and to calm Gina's nervousness.

As the two are walking they are stopped by a crewman. "The two of you need to remain in your room, no one is allowed out at this time."

"What? What are you talking about?" Asks Gina.

"Ma'am we have sick passengers on the ship and we can't risk anymore passengers getting sick." States the crewman.

"We feel fine, but what kind of sickness? What's wrong and why haven't we docked yet?" Asks a concerned Gregory.

The crewman looks at Gregory annoyed and says, "Listen man if I were you, I'd turn on the television in your cabin."

Gregory and Gina look at one another, then hurry back

to their room. The television had not been on since they boarded the ship as they wanted 'alone time'.

Once the television is on, it doesn't take long to see what is going on. A deadly virus has entered the world and people are getting sick by contact. No one knows the type of vaccine needed for this virus or how to effectively stop the spread. All they know is that it is deadly and you must quarantine from others for several days.

Gina walks up to the phone and calls the cabin crew. "Hello, my name is Gina. My husband and I are guests on the cruise and well what does this virus have to do with us not docking? We were supposed to dock 24 hours ago. I have to return to work in the morning and so does my husband. We need to get off this boat."

"Ma'am," says the operator. "No one is allowed off the ship as officials don't know who has the virus and they don't want to risk others getting sick because of people on this ship. We are hoping to hear something soon. Please be patient and in the meantime, we have free drinks in the bar for all guests."

Gina hangs up the phone. "This is absurd. We are stuck on this ship because of some virus? This makes no sense."

Gregory, who has been watching the news while his wife was on the phone says, "That explains why we were sick, this virus has been going around. We would know that if we watched television prior to leaving! It's all over the news!"

"So, this is my fault? Just because I didn't want to be distracted on my honeymoon? I mean our honeymoon?" Cries Gina.

Gregory walks up to his wife and hugs her. "It isn't anyone's fault dear, well at least not ours. Look, lets go down and enjoy free drinks."

Gregory and Gina leave their room and proceed toward the bar. They take the 'scenic' route as Gina wants to feel the breeze of the ocean.

As soon as Gregory opens the door to the exterior of the ship Gina notices that the ship is stopped; at a dock.

"This doesn't make sense, why are we docked? The crew member said we couldn't, this makes no sense." Says Gina with a bit of confusion.

A crew member spots Gina and her husband and yells out, "Go inside, go inside right now."

Gregory is now confused. "Look man I don't know

what's going on but my wife and I will get off here. We can rent a car and drive back home once we get on land…"

Before Gregory could finish his statement, another crewman came out and demanded the couple go inside as this was not a stop for passengers.

Gregory and Gina are escorted back to their room. They are confused and upset. Gina attempts to contact the cruise operator but no answer. She then tries to call her mother but there is no signal.

"Honey," says Gina looking at her husband. "Is your phone working? The cabin phone isn't."

Gregory checks his phone but there is no signal, he grabs his wife's cell phone but again no luck with a signal.

It begins to get late and the two are tired. They lay in bed and fall asleep in one another's arms.

The next morning Gina tries making contact by phone but has no luck. She then remembers her friend from high school being on board.

"That's it," screams Gina. "I need to go to the information desk and try to get in touch with Brenda, she's here on a girl's trip. Maybe one of their phones are working or they have more information on what's going on. Brenda told me she has kids so I know she has been making contact with them and she may have more insight on what exactly is going on."

Gregory informs his wife he will go with her and the two proceed to the information desk.

Once they get there Gina proceeds to speak with the clerk at the desk. "Hi, can you tell me what room Brenda is in?"

"I am sorry ma'am we don't have anyone on the ship by that name." The clerk states after briefly checking the directory.

"Oh wait." Gina thinks for a second. "Brenda Townsman, sorry her full name is Brenda Townsman she boarded the ship the same day as my husband and I, what cabin is she in, we are friends."

The clerk looks through the directory. "As stated, we have no one on the ship by that name, the two of you need to return to your room unless you are going to the bar, that is the only area that is not off limits at this time."

Gina now has both hands planted on her hips. "Ok so you mean to tell me that no one named Brenda is on your list? I saw her. *She is* on your list. Can I see your list?"

The clerk is turning red as she is upset at Gina's behavior and questioning. "Ma'am as I said, I have no one by that name. Please don't make me call security."

Gina is now equally upset. "Please call security, I want you to call fucking security and maybe they can find my friends' room! In fact, let me call them for you, *SECURITY! SECURITY! SECURITY!"*

The clerk picks up the phone and calls security as Gina is screaming on the top of her lungs. Gregory tries to calm her down but she is very upset at this point and her husband's efforts are not making things any better.

Within a few moments, security arrives. The clerk alerts them of Gina's irate behavior after discovering no one by the name of 'Brenda' is on board.

"Ma'am, sir, you both need to return to your cabin." Security warns in a stern tone.

"Look here man," says Gina. "I only need to get in touch with Brenda that's all. I am not trying to cause trouble. How is it that she doesn't have all of her cruise attendants in her directory? That makes no sense, are you going to help or do I need to knock on every single cabin door of this ship?'

"That's enough," shouts security. "Back to your room *NOW*."

Gregory while standing near his wife tries to be the voice of reason. "Listen we are not trouble makers my wife just wants to talk with her friend, if you can't give the room number that is totally understandable. Can you at least call her room and ask her to meet us in the bar? We can wait for her there and we won't bother you all any longer."

The security guard and clerk give each other a 'look.' The clerk then says, "This is my last time telling you both, there is no Brenda on this ship. Brenda is a very easy name to remember, common name actually, if she and her friends were on this cruise ship, I'd know! Now as I said there is no Brenda aboard. You have two options: leave and return to your room or be personally escorted to the 'holding' cell of the ship for disturbing the peace. The choice is yours; I suggest you choose wisely."

"What is your name? I am making a complaint.' States

Gregory.

The clerk looks at Gregory and laughs. "Making a complaint, you are funny, but if you think that will help go ahead my name is Karen."

Gregory, now pissed by the way the clerk and security is handling this, opens his mouth to say something when Gina interrupts him and says, "Let's go dear."

Gregory looks at her in shock but walks off with her. The two silently walk back to their cabin.

"Really Gina, that's it? You start this then just leave and walk off like everything is okay? I saw you talk with Brenda and her friends. They were on the ship. They boarded and they had luggage. Brenda even stated it was a girl's trip! They are on this ship why would you just want to walk away like that?" Gregory asks as he demands answers from his wife.

Gina looks at her husband as if she'd seen a ghost "Key word Gregory, *friends*."

"Huh? What," asks Gregory.

Gina looks at her husband and again says "friends." Gina shakes her head. "The clerk said Brenda and her friends were never on the ship. But I never mentioned

Brenda being with friends. I never said if she was alone or with a husband or kids, I only asked for Brenda."

Gregory is now shocked. "You are right! You are absolutely right! I never caught that but you are correct. But why? Why lie about her not being on the ship if she knows she is here with friends? What's so secretive about her being here. I mean she didn't even try to call her room she just said she isn't here; like she just never existed on this ship. This is so weird. First, we can't dock because of some virus and now this? Too weird."

The couple tries to rationalize what is occurring but they can't. They are now coming up on 48 hours being on a ship that was supposed to dock and now Brenda and possibly her friends are missing. And to make matters worse they have no working phone lines because they are too far off at sea to get a signal.

Within a few hours the couple decides to watch television and agree to try and make more sense of everything in the morning.

While watching television the news is constantly speaking of this virus. A virus with no vaccine that can be caught simply by walking too close to someone.

"Change the channel," says Gina. "This is too

depressing." Gregory flips the channel and sees an emergency alert on the television.

NEWSFLASH EMERGENCY ALERT: *'The police would like to thank everyone for the calls over the last 24 hours. Suspicious activity was reported by the boating dock. Though we found no evidence that leads to a suspect, we did find clues that we are hoping the community can come forward and help us with identifying possible missing person(s).'*

The news shows several pictures. Nothing alarming to Gregory but Gina sits straight up with her hand over her mouth. "Oh my God. Oh my God. That purse, that purse, oh my God."

Gina notices Brenda's new limited purse; pink with the gray straps. The exact new handbag that literally just came out in stores and it's now found at a docking port!?!

Gina starts to think back. The ship just docked somewhere but the crewman made her and Gregory return to their room.

What is going on? Brenda is missing, her friends are possibly missing and everyone is stuck aboard the ship because of a virus.

"We have to get out of here," says Gina.

"Gina," says Gregory who was also lost in thought. "We are on a cruise ship in the middle of the ocean we can't just 'get out of here' that is not how this works!"

"Well, I can't stay here. There is no phone and like seriously who can we trust on this ship? Clearly, Karen the clerk and security guard are involved in whatever the hell is going on. Did you see the way they looked at one another? And how she said Brenda's name, like didn't tell him a last name just the first name like as to say you know the '*Brenda*' that we just killed. Oh my God they killed her. They killed her and what if we are next, we know too much they may kill us." Says Gina with tears in her eyes.

Gregory embraces Gina with a warm hug. "Calm down, no one said anything about anyone on this ship being murdered, relax."

Gregory is questioning what could have happened in his head and though he does suspect foul play he doesn't want his new wife to be worried.

Time passes. It has now been eight long days that the couple, along with guests, have been on the cruise ship. The boat is not allowed to dock because of this deadly virus with no vaccine and to make it worse the cruise ship is running low on toilet paper. The ship usually restocks when they dock but since they were not allowed to properly dock, the ship only has what was already on board. Food buffets are now limited to set times with only one plate of food. Restrooms are starting to smell and get clogged. Passengers have to stay a few feet apart from one another and sanitize frequently and to make matters worse the bar is out of alcohol.

Gregory and Gina are miserable.

"I can't take this. I just can't. I am going out for air," says Gina.

"NO," screams Gregory. "You know the rules, you don't want to get sick and besides all they will do is escort you back in the room."

"For one we were already sick, remember after the wedding? They said we had the flu? I bet we had that virus and didn't even know it. So technically we already dealt with it and survived. *I am getting out of here!"* Gina slams the door and walks out.

Gregory puts on his shoes in a hurry and storms after his wife. Surprisingly he doesn't see her even though she just ran out a few seconds ago.

Gregory walks past the stairway but still doesn't see her. He then proceeds to turn around, thinking she may have gone the other way when all of a sudden, he hears a male's voice.

"What do we do with her? We just got the official word that we can dock and let passengers quarantine at a vacant hotel on land but we can't let her dock. She knows that Brenda and the other ladies boarded. She's going to be trouble; I can feel it."

Gregory peeps inside and he can see two people standing talking to one another. He doesn't see his wife anywhere but is certain they either have her or they know of her whereabouts, as the two people in the room are Karen the clerk and the security guard from days ago when the couple first inquired of Brenda.

Gregory doesn't want to leave the area as he knows his wife couldn't have gone far and must be in that room, but he hears footsteps. He races to his room and closes the door. He tries to use his cell phone but there is no signal. He picks up the cabin phone; nothing.

He is confused at this point. He knows they have his wife but what can he do! The room where he overheard the conversation is not far from his room so he stays near the door as he thinks he will be able to notice when they leave the room.

Gregory is sitting with his ear to the door. After hours of nothing, he decides to leave the room. He steps out but before turning the corner he sees two large guards talking. He turns around and returns to the room. Gregory believes that they were sent to 'watch' him from coming out and complaining of his wife being gone from the room.

Gregory remembers that on one of the first nights at sea Gina would stand and watch the ocean from the oversized window in their room. Gregory decides that his only option is to try to escape the room from the window and somehow attempt to get to the exit of the boat in case they tried to drop Gina off at a nearby dock in route to the passenger docking location.

Gregory tries his hardest to fit through the window but he is unsuccessful. He then ties blankets together and unplugs the TV. He places the TV inside the blankets and wraps it as tight as he can. He then goes to the window and throws the wrapped TV out the window hoping it will create a loud sound and cause everyone to go outside.

Gregory drops the TV wrapped in blankets. To his surprise it is louder than expected. Within seconds he hears the sounds of footsteps. Unsure if they saw which room it came from, he hides briefly behind the door in case the guards near the door entered his room. No one enters. He then peeks out the window, hiding from being seen. He sees several of the guests outside including the guards that were near his door along with the crewmen. They are unsure if a person fell aboard and are trying to be sure everyone is safe.

Gregory runs out of the room. There is one 'dock' exit that passengers go through so he is certain that if he can get to it, he can see if they remove his wife off the ship.

Gregory successfully makes it near the exit. There aren't many places to hide so he finds a small linen closet within a few feet of the exit. Gregory enters and after hours of waiting falls asleep inside the closet.

A short time after he is awakened by the sounds of the clerk talking. "I know, I know this wasn't part of the original plan but it works in your favor. You get another one for half the price. However, I will be upfront you may not get much for her because she is black. She is a little 'feisty' so be prepared. We gave her something but I don't know how much longer it'll keep her sassy ghetto ass sedated."

Gregory is certain Karen is speaking of his wife Gina. But why? Why are they getting rid of her and to who? Gregory is confused but remains calm and focused.

Within a few minutes Gregory witnesses the two guards that were near his door escorting a person covered in a brown sheet. Gregory looks at the feet and knows that it is Gina based off her shoes. It's the same shoes he purchased her for her birthday because the color of the shoes matched the color of his favorite football team.

"What about the husband?" Questions one guard to another as they walk by.

"He didn't leave the room." Says the other guard. "He must be asleep which is perfect. A few minutes before we dock, we will go in and make sure he stays asleep. Don't worry, because of the virus no one will come and check the ship once passengers get off so we have time to discard him when we go back at sea; we have everything covered."

The two men walk off of the boat with the person who Gregory without a doubt realizes is Gina.

Gregory is very careful as he is unsure if the clerk or

anyone else is nearby. He exits the linen closet and can hear line music playing, "Well I be damn," thought Gregory. "That's the same music that was played the night Gina and I were caught questioning the reason the boat stopped at a dock. It must be music to get everyone dancing and distracted."

Gregory almost makes it completely off the ship when he hears a noise. He ducks down as low as he can hoping and praying that they didn't see him. He looks up a few seconds later and no one is there. Gregory is now off the ship. The only problem is he doesn't know where they took Gina. The sun is setting and he has no clue as to where he is but he knows the two guards have to get back on the boat before it sails off. Gregory looks around but stays close to where the boat is. After ten minutes or so he witnesses the guards walking and laughing. Gina is not with them. Once the two men board the ship Gregory walks near the area that he suspects his wife to be.

There is a small shed-like building; windows are covered so you can't see inside. The building appears abandoned and is sitting on bricks. There are no cars in the area. Nobody seemingly around.

Gregory begins to fear the worse. Believing that his

wife has been killed he takes a moment to gather his thoughts.

The door to the shed is locked with a padlock. The windows are boarded. Gregory walks around to the back. There is a back door with a key entry. Gregory looks around outside for something to break in the shed.

His attempts are unsuccessful at first but after walking around the area he finds large amounts of wood. He is determined to get to Gina as he is certain that she is inside. After what seems like forever, he is able to open the door. It is dark inside and there are no lights. He stumbles around and sees Gina's shoes. His heart is beating heavy. He walks up to the brown blanket she is covered in and takes a deep breath. He slowly pulls off the blanket and there she is; Gina is right before his eyes.

Gina, to his surprise, is alive and awake. There is gray tape over her mouth and her hands are tied behind her back. Gregory rips off the tape and Gina gasps for air before crying hysterically. Gina then whispers; "They are coming."

Gregory, while taking off the ties from her hands says, "No one is coming they left, they are back on the ship."

"No," cries Gina between tears. "The buyers are coming".

Gregory looks at his wife but before he can say anything the sounds of a car is heard driving closer to the shed.

"Get up, hurry, can you walk? We have to leave now." Says a very frightened Gregory.

Gina is able to stand, though she wobbles a bit. Her husband grabs her by the hand.

"Wait." Gregory looks at his wife. "Where is your friend? Where is Brenda, we can't just leave her and her friends here."

"No one else is here, we have to go. I heard the guys talking while they were tying me. The buyers come right after the bodies are brought here." Gina whispers while crying her eyes out.

Gregory and Gina walk out of the back door and the couple race into the wooded area. The newlyweds run until they reach safety.

Once to safety Gina journals her thoughts….

Where are they now? You see the pictures posted daily. Some young others old. Blacks with many whites. They come from all walks of life, many different locations and cultures. All people who woke up and left home but never returned. What happened? Certainly, someone knows? How is it that families are constantly getting faced with closed doors? They left without a trace, just disappeared in the night yet the world keeps moving as though everything is alright. Who is responsible? Where do we start? This tragedy is tearing the world apart. Have you seen her? Where did he go? Surely somehow, someone must know.

Family Secrets

Hi! I'm Ezekiel but everyone calls me Zeke. I have what every kid around me wishes they had; the perfect family. My mom, Karen, is a counselor. She loves helping people and believes that as long as you do good things for people you like you will live a happy life. I am an only child but I am never bored because my dad (Timothy) is so cool. He plays basketball with me every evening until it's time for dinner and we have swimming competitions together in the backyard all the time. We live in this amazing house and I have a dog named 'Oscar'. I am currently in the 5th grade and the lead reader in the youth bible study group at church. I like going to church but sometimes the lessons are above my head, hopefully as the time passes, I can fully understand the bible and be able to interpret it more easily. Oh, and guess what? Dad said we are going on a vacation soon. I am hoping that mom and dad allow me to bring a friend on vacation, that would be so cool. Wow my life is perfect, well at least it was. It's funny how one knock on the door can change your entire life……….

"Mom I can't find my blue socks." I yell as I began looking for my favorite tennis shoes. "Did you check the dryer? I washed socks yesterday and I am certain I saw your blue socks with the other items." Shouts my mom.

I rush down the stairs to the laundry room and there it is, my favorite blue socks. These are the socks I wore when I passed my math test. I also wore them when I gave Amber my eraser (but don't tell my mom she thinks I keep forgetting my eraser at school). Blue is my favorite color and everyone who knows me knows if you want to make me smile; buy me something blue.

"Ezekiel, hurry up your dad will be off from work any minute, we have to meet him for dinner to celebrate his promotion at work." Shouts mom.

"Can I call Jay to see if his parents will allow him to come with us? That way I can have company while you and dad talk during dinner?" I ask in a pleading voice.

Mom, is now standing with her right hand on her hip. "No, and don't ever ask me that again. He nor his parents are allowed in this house or in our presence ever again.'

"But Mom." I whine.

In a very stern voice mom says, "Zeke we have been

through this before. Jay is going to be gay and I can't have him rubbing off his ways on you. It's bad enough he lives with two of the same sex parents. I should have called child welfare services when I found out about that disgusting situation. I Know technically it's not Jay's fault but well, the fact that he is black is already a problem and well, oh never mind, you will understand when you are older but for now stay away from that boy and his family. Let's get going Lord knows I almost lost my appetite just thinking about those freaks."

"Mom why do we have to go out to dinner every time dad gets a promotion? Like seriously this is his third promotion in two months. He should let someone else get recognized, don't you think?" I ask mom.

Mom looks at me with a smirk, her index finger pointing and waving sarcastically. "So, do you want me to call and cancel your private school tuition? Or how about I call the pool guy and tell him we no longer need the swimming pool in the back yard, or what about…."

"Mom." I shout. "I get the picture. Dad makes a lot of money when he gets these promotions. Geesh, I love my swimming pool, besides one night of dinner doesn't sound so bad after all."

Suddenly Oscar starts barking at the sound of the doorbell ringing.

"I will get the door mom, are you expecting guests? I thought it was only us three going out to dinner." I shout as I finished putting on my socks.

I run to the door and to my surprise is a tall man carrying a blue basketball.

The man is about six feet tall. He is slender and his hands are shaking. In fact, he is sweating and he looks really scared.

"Who's at the door Ezekiel?" Asks mom as she walks towards the doorway. Just as she walks to the doorway the man looks at me and says, "Hello son."

I must be hearing things, did this man just call be s-son? Like as in a boy? Ok yeah that makes sense.

"What are you doing here Joseph?" Asks my mom angrily as she approached the door.

"Umm mom is this a friend of yours? How do you know his name?" I ask as I am very confused.

My mom looks at me and instructs me to go upstairs to my room. But just as I turn away to go upstairs the man touches my shoulder and says, "No, he is *MY* son and I want to visit with him."

"You have absolutely no right to show up to my home and make demands. We agreed that you would never ever come here. How dare you come here? What is wrong with you? *WHY ARE YOU HERE? I NEED YOU TO LEAVE IMMEDIATELY AND NEVER RETURN.*" Mom shouts in a tone in which I had never heard her speak.

"Can I come in?" Asks the man.

"Hell No," states my mom. She then slams the door.

"Mom, what is going on? I don't understand what is…" before I could finish my statement my mom looks me in the eyes and says, "This conversation is over! And we will never speak of this again."

I am confused, shocked, and very worried. I have never witnessed this side of my mom and well is it true? Is my dad not my dad? I have pictures with him since I was a baby and he calls me his son and, this just makes absolutely no sense. And what's worse is my mom is acting so strange.

"Zeke," yells Karen. "Let's go we will be late."

I run towards her as fast as I can. She has the car keys in her hand and we leave the house. It is the longest car ride ever. Dead silence. No music, no talking, just a long drawn silent ride.

We arrive to this very fancy restaurant. The valet greets us and we go inside.

"Hello we have reservations for three." My mom states as she gives the hostess our reservation information.

We are escorted to a table overlooking a beautiful courtyard. Dad, well I mean I think he's my dad, hasn't made it yet. I want to try to forget the whole random visitor that was at our house but I can't, I just keep waiting for my mom to say something, anything to let me know what was going on, but she says nothing.

The waitress comes to our table and brings us fresh bread and water. My mom orders an entire bottle of wine in celebration of my dad's promotion along with oysters as a sampler while we await dad's arrival. Within five minutes or so, dad arrives. He greets mom with a kiss and pats my head as he always does. He and mom discuss his recent promotion while I sit and stared at him. I wonder if he knew that I was not his, was he there for my birth? I want to ask questions but I know soon as I do my mom will change the subject and later scold me for bringing up what happened this evening. Then again maybe I'm his and the man who came over to the house was crazy; yep, that's it, that's the story I'm going with. The other guy is tripping because there is no way my mom would keep such a thing from me. I will never bring it up again. Life is great. Dad just got a promotion. I love everything I have and most of all if I keep quiet maybe I can guilt mom into buying me the new video game that is releasing next week. It's settled. Life is good and I am not going to change that!

Shortly after the waitress returns to take our order. Mom orders stuffed seafood with pasta, dad orders a steak well done with mashed potatoes and I order my favorite which is jambalaya with chicken, sausage, and shrimp; yummy.

"How was your day son?" Dad asks me.

"Umm it was ok I guess." I answer nervously.

"Zeke," says dad with a puzzled look. "Are you ok? What's wrong?"

My mom looks at me with her eye brows raised and says, "He's fine, he was upset because he wanted the new video game that comes out next week but I told him no on the way here but you know what, he deserves it, so tomorrow after work we can go and reserve your game for when it comes out, *OK son*!"

"Umm o-ok mom, thanks." I say as I am in shock of her response.

"Awesome." Dad says with a grin. "I get a promotion and you get a new video game."

He and mom then laugh. I pretend to be happy but all I could do is stare at dad.

Apparently, dad caught me staring at him as he stops laughing and says, "Zeke, you look like you seen a ghost, are you sure you are ok?"

Mom interrupts yet again. "He is fine, he had a long day at school. We may have to end the dinner a little early so that he can go home and rest up for school, after all we have another long day tomorrow. We have to go to the store and reserve his video game and then I have grocery to purchase. Zeke, baby you know the peach cobbler you've been begging me to bake? I will bake it for you tomorrow night, K?"

"Thanks mom." I say with a smile. I absolutely love her peach cobbler. It is the best in the whole world. You know, I can get used of this. A new video game, homemade cobbler, wow my life is amazing.

Dinner arrives to our table shortly after. It is delicious. The three of us talk about our next vacation spot and dad informs us about the details of his promotion.

The waitress later returns to our table. "Hello, would you all like to try dessert? Today's special is Apple Strudel. Anyone have room for something sweet?"

"ARE YOU MY REAL DAD?" I blurt, while staring at my dad.

The waitress, mom, and dad looked at me as though the world has just ended.

"I-I will um I will be right back I think I forgot my pen in the kitchen." Says the waitress as she leaves our table abruptly.

Mom, being the quick thinker that she is says, "Zeke, dear, of course he is your dad. I think you are exhausted and it's clearly time to go."

"I'm sorry, I just can't get the man calling me son out of my head and…"

I was stopped by my dad as he says sternly, *"WHAT MAN?!"*

I look over at my mom who is red with anger. "Mom I am so sorry I just really want to know who he was, he called me son, and I heard how you talked to him, it's like he angered you for coming over to the house, I just want to know what's going on."

"He came over to whose house, Karen what is going on," asks dad.

"This isn't the time or place. Let's go home and we can talk there." Mom says in a somewhat annoyed tone.

Dad agrees as an open restaurant is not the ideal place to have such a private discussion.

Dad pays the bill. Needless to say, we never stayed long enough to order dessert.

The car ride going home is longer than on the way there. Dad actually is in the car with mom and I as he had his business partner drop him to the restaurant earlier.

I feel so bad for blurting it out the way I did. There was so much tension in the car.

No one spoke, the radio was off, dad was driving extremely fast which he only does when he is trying to rush to get somewhere. It was very awkward.

We finally return home. I attempt to walk towards my room, in case they needed to 'talk' first but I am instructed by dad to have a seat in the living room.

Mom isn't happy. She thought the two of them should talk first but per dad 'there has clearly been too many side conversations already.'

Dad looks at me, smiles, and takes a deep breath. "You will always be my son. Nothing will ever change that. I remember the day you were born. It was the happiest day of my life. You were such a big baby." Dad chuckles. "After looking at you for the first time I promised you that I would give you the world. Your birth motivated me to be the person I am today. I worked so hard to give you everything you wanted and needed. You, son, are my pride and joy. I will always be your dad, but well, your mom has something that she needs to tell you."

Mom is sitting in tears. She looks at me then turns away.

After a few moments, between drying her tears, she begins to talk.

"When I was younger, before I met your dad, I was involved in a relationship that wasn't healthy. The man that I was with, wasn't ready to be a father, hell he wasn't even ready to be a boyfriend. He had multiple women and a bad temper; though he never physically abused me, he came very close when he found out I was pregnant. He was young and made it clear he didn't want to be a father. He just wanted to have fun. When he left me, I told him he'd never see his son again because he was not about to be in and out of our lives whenever he felt like it. He left before you were born. There I was pregnant, with no man and no direction. A few months later, while still pregnant, I met Timothy. He and I just clicked, we briefly dated and he accepted me and more importantly he accepted you. Before you were even born, he accepted that you were not his but soon as he looked into your eyes his heart grew for you. Timothy and I married and the three of us became a family. Truth is, I never thought in a trillion years that your real father, Joseph would return. I still don't even know how he found us or why after all these years he feels he can just walk back into your life. Joseph is your biological father, but Timothy is your dad."

I have no words to say, I would have never thought that our perfect family wasn't perfect. I don't really know how to feel.

"I, umm, is it okay if I go lay down? I am very tired." I

say in a very low tone.

My parents agree that we have had enough conversation for one night.

I retire to my bed for the night but I never slept. Tears continuously flow from my eyes. I am still shocked and slightly confused. I have no idea what will happen now, or if any of this will change anything. I mean Joseph may never come back and there is a chance that life will return to normal.

The next morning mom wakes me up for school as normal. She tries to act as though last night didn't exist. Not one word of it is spoken.

The school day is long and boring. I return home and it is just as though last night never happened. Dad and I play outside, mom cooked dinner and even bakes my favorite cobbler. We didn't reserve my game today because the line was extremely long at the game store and mom was too tired to wait; but she said we can go tomorrow.

Weeks go by and things are seemingly back to normal.

"Oh, my goodness," says mom. "Timothy, look dear, your favorite movie is playing on TV."

Dad filled with excitement says to me, "Turn the TV up, Zeke you will love this movie. It is incredible."

I walk over to the television and the three of us begin to watch the movie.

About twenty minutes into the movie the doorbell rings.

"I got it." Says dad who is already standing from popping popcorn.

"Who's at the door dear," asks mom. "Is it someone selling cookies again? If so, I need two boxes of anything sweet."

Dad walks back to the TV area, to my surprise right behind him is the guy from the other night; my father.

Mom leaps up. "What is going on, why are you here? You need to leave."

"Wait, look Zeke knows and I can't go through life wondering what would have happened if we would have just tried to hear Joseph out. We are adults. Let's get some closure so that we all can move on." Timothy says with a stern voice while extending his hand towards the sofa so that Joseph can have a seat.

As for me I am now sitting very close to my mom.

Joseph, who is sitting across from us ponders his thoughts before speaking. "I am not here to cause trouble. I just, well, there is no easy way to say this. Look I made some mistakes, I'll admit that. But I am older now, we all are and I want to be in my son's life. I know, before you say anything, trust me I know that things will take time and I can't just come in here and I am not in a position to make demands but I want to be involved. It doesn't have to be every day, we can start on weekends, I just want to be in my son's life."

"You're right," states mom. "You can't just come in here and make demands. You need to leave. *NOW*."

"Karen, I am trying, trying to have a relationship with *OUR* son. Please don't make this harder than it has to be," says Joseph.

"Zeke doesn't need another father, he has one." Says mom while grinding her teeth. "Get out, and I don't know how you found us but try to forget this address just as you forgot about your son when you walked out years ago!"

My dad, Timothy is now standing beside my mom. "You need to leave. Karen has clearly made her mind up."

Joseph with a smirk says, "Made her mind up? This isn't her choice. Ezekiel isn't some charity case that Karen can dictate the outcome. He is my son. *MY* son. I never gave up parental rights. I have never been a danger to my son hell I have never in life had so much as a late bill, I handle my business. There is no judge in the world that would give you full custody and not take into consideration that I deserve to be in my son's life. I came here to try to work it out without bringing in the courts, but if that's how you want it? Fuck it. Mark my words I will see you in court. Oh, and for the record, I live two hours away. I own a home; have a good job and I have the finances to take care of *MY* son. You want to fight me? Let's fight. If we go through the courts, I will petition the court for joint custody which means every other weekend, holiday, summer, and any time that the court sees fit I will have my son with me!"

Joseph then proceeds to walk out before mom stops him.

"Joseph, look this is all too much. I mean it's been years and you just want us to change everything that's normal to us in a second's notice? Look, you said you live a few hours away, right? Against my better judgment, I think we should all at least sit down and have dinner together. I'll cook, no restaurant. Let's just all sit down and plan a date when we can figure out how to proceed. We need to do what's best for everyone; especially Zeke."

Joseph is silent for a moment. "I am free Saturday, is that enough time to get a dinner together?"

Mom and dad look at each other in agreement. Mom says, "Yes, definitely."

"Is it okay if I bring someone? I'm married and I want us all to be able to get to know one another, if that's okay with you; if not I understand as this is plenty to take in as it is."

My dad reaches out his hand to Joseph. "We will see you both Saturday evening. Dinner will be ready at 6pm."

Dad and Joseph shake hands. Then dad walks Joseph out the door.

Mom looks at me. In a very comforting voice she asks, "Are you okay? Do you want to discuss your feelings son?"

I embrace mom and I give her a big warm hug. "I am fine mom. I only have one request. Can you make peach cobbler again for dessert Saturday?"

Mom giggles a bit and tickles me. "You bet I can son."

Saturday seems to take forever to arrive. I didn't really know how I was feeling. I mean I am happy to know the truth and I don't think it will be bad to get to know Joseph. I just know I am not ready to go anywhere with him or spend the night at his home. I mean technically he is a stranger to me. But I know my mom will help figure everything out. As long as Joseph understands that it will take time for everyone to adjust, this new normal may not be as bad as I thought.

Mom began cooking dinner early on Saturday to be sure everything would be ready in time. She prepared meatloaf, cornbread dressing, broccoli casserole, and for dessert my favorite; peach cobbler. She had a bottle of wine and whiskey on the table along with unsweet tea. Mom hardly ever puts whiskey on the dinner table. She only drinks whiskey when she wants to 'slip away' from reality.

Dad on the other hand was chill. He said that we all just need to relax. He said a dinner at home is actually a nice thing to do. It's in a comfortable environment and will help everyone get to know each other better.

The doorbell rings. Mom takes a deep breath then instructs my dad to open the door.

There he is, my birth father, on the other side of the door. I take a deep breath. I know he is married and won't be alone but I want to keep my focus on Joseph.

Dad opens the door while mom and I stand near him to welcome our guests inside. Mom wants them to know that they are welcomed so she wanted us all at the door smiling to lighten the mood.

Dad opens the door.

Dad, mom, and I all stand there with each of our mouth wide open.

Mom who is never speechless, says nothing.

Dad pulls himself together and welcomes our guests inside our home.

"Please, please do come in. The dining room table is straight ahead on the right." Says dad as he nudges mom.

We all walk to the dinner table.

Dad takes the lead to jumpstart the conversation. "So, the weather, it's nice and um you know um Karen she prepared this beautiful meal for everyone tonight, um so um Joseph, how are you? How did the two of you meet one another?"

All eyes are on Joseph. "Well, it's quite interesting really. So, a few years ago, I was sent here for work, well technically two hours away from here but anyway, the two of us met while I was having dinner at a restaurant. I was all alone because I had never been to the area. It was my last night in town so I wanted to just get out and relax you know, nothing big just dinner and chill time. To my surprise I wasn't the only one eating alone that night. It was weird because everyone in the restaurant was with a guest but there the two of us were, almost directly across one another at different tables; alone. We locked eyes. I almost instantly fell in love. And well, to be honest the rest is history. Oh, and for the record, just in case you all are wondering, I made the first move that night."

Mom pretends to find it funny as she uses her fake laugh. Dad just grins and well I don't do anything. I am utterly confused and shocked.

"I'm sorry." Says mom after taking a drink of whiskey. "We didn't catch your name."

"My apologies, I can't believe Joseph didn't tell you all my name. Joseph told me about you three. He has been talking about you all nonstop since he first came here.

He was so excited to see his son and well I guess with all of the excitement he forgot to properly introduce me. I am so happy to finally meet you all, my name is Marvin."

Joseph is not just married, but he is married to a black man. My real father is married, gay, and my step-father is black!

I am unsure how I am required to feel right now. I am sitting with my mouth open unable to speak. I just keep trying to get my mind to understand what my eyes are witnessing.

I don't want to seem rude but this is a very awkward dinner.

I have never had actual conversations with gay people in real life. How do I talk to them? What happens if I stare? Do they think I am different or is it that they are the ones that are unique? I mean I do go on the internet and sometimes gay people are seen on the television but mom makes me change the channel, and well my friend Jay lives with gay parents but mom says that's not normal and I shouldn't be around any of that.

So now what? I can't change the channel; I can't act like gay people don't exist. I clearly can't just ignore it.

Is this really happening? What do I do? How do I address this? My biological father is married to a black man and now they want to be part of my life.

Where do we go from here?

After a few years pass by Ezekiel journals his thoughts....

This is the new normal. There are some things that you can never change. But we all have a choice; we can accept what is or dwell in regret of what will never be. One thing is for sure we must allow each person the opportunity to be free. Free to love whomever they choose; if not in the end you will lose. Don't miss memories or close the door simply because you don't agree with the life they live. Be free to see beneath what appears and love one another the best way you know how. Love one another with no shame and no judgement. Take the time to open your glasses lens, it is then that you will see that true love wins.

We Woke Up

Generational Curse

"Dammit Donna, take off those headphones and listen to me. I will be late tonight. You are 21 years old. I should not have to tell you this but, be sure and set the alarm when you leave and please turn off the lights. Last time you forgot. We are new to this neighborhood. I don't really know everyone so I need the alarm set nightly, especially since you aren't home regularly. Donna, are you listening?"

Donna who clearly is not paying any attention to her mother (Tina) replies, "Yea sure whatever you say mom."

Tina walks out as she is leaving to attend a late-night dinner with friends.

Meanwhile Donna continues listening to music. She prepares herself a turkey sandwich with lettuce and cheese then walks toward the backyard to get fresh air.

To her surprise the neighbor, a young woman seemingly close to Donna's age is outside in her own yard.

"Hey, hey, come here," yells Donna.

 The young woman looks around then walks over to Donna who is now fully laid out on the patio lawn with her turkey sandwich in hand.

"Hi, I'm Donna, we just moved here, well technically I live on campus but anyway like I said, I'm Donna."

The young lady seems surprisingly shy. She lifts up her right hand and waves but says nothing.

Donna is now sitting in awkwardness. "So, um have you lived here long? Any cute guys around here?"

The young lady looks back, then slowly begins to speak. "I have lived here my entire life. It's a quiet neighborhood. Nice to meet you." She then walks away.

Donna bursts out laughing. She then, under her breath whispers, "weirdo."

Donna finishes her turkey sandwich and enjoys the late evening breeze while listening to music.

Later Donna locks her mothers' home, sets the alarm and drives back to her campus dorm room where she lives (most of the time).

Donna, a junior in college loves all things researchable.

She aspires to one day be a crime lab detective but for now only pretends to be one.

Once Donna had questions about her dorm roommate merely because of the fact her roommate's family never visited. Donna waited until her roommate slept, went through her belongings and took a photo of her license. She then began 'researching' her. Donna used the address from the license to locate the family living there hoping they would either be related to her roommate or know of her family. Well, come to find out the address was that of her roommate's grandfather who happened to be a retired principal. He raised her roommate after the death of her mother. She never knew her father and was an only child. The only reason the grandfather never visited the college was because he doesn't drive anymore. But he purchased the roommate a car so she could travel home every other weekend to see him. Once Donna's roommate found out what she had done, she requested a room change calling Donna a 'psycho.'

Donna now has her own room, which she hates, particularly it is why she spends a lot of time at her mom's house.

Because the Christmas holidays are near Donna knew it

would be a great time to get a much-needed break and relax at her mothers' new home. She attended her final class, packed her clothes and prepared for the ride home for the holidays.

The ride was long and boring. Donna's mother is from the bayou and though they lived much of their lives in the city once Donna graduated high school her mom said she always wanted to go back to 'her roots'. It took time, three years actually, for her mother to find the 'right' house. She needed to be sure it was a home she could help raise her grandchildren, one day retire at, and later leave to her own kids. Donna has an older brother; he isn't home much as he and his wife live in a different state. Donna wasn't ever too fond of the 'country living' in fact she hates the south. According to her mom Donna hasn't given it a chance but Donna's issue is that it is boring and nothing to 'investigate'. Nothing but cotton fields, long roads, trees, and wild animals. The only positivity that Donna could think of is the fact that it is peaceful.

After several hours of driving Donna finally arrives.

"Guess who's back." Yells Donna as she opens the front door.

"I am in the dining room," replies Tina.

Donna walks in the area to greet her mom but to her surprise her mom has the entire Christmas tree and decorations laid out. Donna is looking disgusted. "Mother, please tell me that you do not expect me to spend my holiday break putting up Christmas decorations with you. Like seriously?"

Donna's mom chuckles. "No Donna, I know you hate assisting. Don't worry I got it covered. But I do need you to go in the backyard and get the rest of the lights. I cleaned them and left them out to dry but I need them now."

"You left them out to dry?! You are so country mom." Says Donna as she walks out to the backyard.

To her surprise there are two teenagers playing outside in the yard next door.

"Hello." Shouts Donna.

"Hey, hello." Both teenagers scream back as they wave.

"Hmmm," thought Donna. "They are so much nicer than the girl that was over at that house a few days ago."

Donna goes back inside with the decorations in hand for her mother.

"Mom, have you met the neighbors?" She asks.

Her mom looks up and thinks briefly. "You know, come to think of it I haven't. There is only one semi close house, the rest are driving distance."

"So, how about we go introduce ourselves to the neighbors next door." Suggests Donna.

Tina looks confused. "You want to meet new people? Since when?"

Donna is now rolling her eyes at her mom. "Anyway, I just thought it would be nice to say hi, that's all, so can we go? You know just to say hi that's it. Don't overdo it and get all nice, just a hello and good-bye."

Tina agrees. She and Donna finishes organizing the decorations so that Tina could put them around the house then shortly after they walk over to the neighbor.

"I feel bad," says Tina. "We should have brought something. This is the south you are supposed to bring food."

"But mom," smirks Donna. "We are the new neighbors technically they should bring something to us and they haven't so with that being said; we are good. We can say hello and head back home."

Donna and her mom Tina arrive at the neighbors. After a short wait, the door is opened by the same girl from a few days ago.

Donna recognizes her instantly. "You, I met you and you never really spoke instead you acted shady."

Before she could finish speaking a voice is overheard asking who is at the door.

The girl, not saying a word opens the door wider so that the people inside the house can see Donna and her mom.

A lady, very well-dressed walks up to the door. "I can handle it from here dear." She says to the weird girl who still has not spoken.

"Hello my name is Karen. How may I assist you," asks the woman?

"Hello." Tina now has her arms extended. "I'm Tina and this is my daughter Donna. We just moved here, well I just moved here and well I thought it was only right to come and say hello."

The lady who introduced herself as Karen shakes hands with Tina then says, "Thank you for coming it is so nice to meet you. My husband instructed me to go over a few days ago but well, it's been so busy with the holidays that I haven't been able to get some sweets for you. I do apologize."

"No, no need to apologize, we just came by to say hello, have a happy holiday." Says Tina as she grabs Donna's hand to leave.

Karen is now walking out the door to speak with them. "Listen, I really do feel bad and well it's the holidays, how about you two come back in about an hour and we can sit and have appetizers and get to know one another. I have two daughters, I would love for us all to sit and chat, please after all we are neighbors."

Before Donna can say hell no, as that's what she is thinking, Tina responds. "Sure, we would love it, we will be back in an hour."

Karen re-enters her home. Donna and Tina walk back to their home. The two both freshen up and prepare for appetizers with the neighbors.

"Mom you know what's weird?" Asks Donna. "She said she has two daughters but one girl opened the door and I saw two additional girls in the backyard."

"Well," Tina says, "Maybe one is her step-daughter or a

visiting family member, it is the holidays dear.”

Within an hour Donna and Tina return to the neighbors. They are greeted after ringing the doorbell by the ‘weird’ girl who doesn’t speak. She literally opens the door, nods her head and allows them into the home.

Once in the home, there is a pre-set dining table very close to the front door. Karen along with the two girls that were outside earlier in the day are already seated at the table.

“Welcome ladies.” Karen pleasantly says. “I forgot to ask what you like to eat so we prepared hamburger sliders, boneless wings, egg rolls with spinach, deviled eggs, and shrimp on a stick, I hope you see something you like.”

“To be honest, this looks amazing.” Donna says with a watering mouth.

Everyone at the table laughs.

Donna and Tina join the others at the table. They make small talk. It is discovered that Karen is the head of an engineering firm and her two daughters are sixteen-year-old fraternal twins (Haley and Bailey). Karen and Tina hit it off immediately, both are hard working mothers with two children. And if that's not enough both women were born and raised in the bayou, a place dear to their hearts.

Everyone is talking and eating, actually having a good time when Donna realizes that the 'weird' girl never sat at the table. Not once, she didn't return after opening the door nor was she cordial.

Donna leans over to Karen's daughter Bailey and whispers, "The other girl, um who is she, I mean based off her looks I didn't think she was your sister but,"

Before Donna can finish Karen notices her whispering and says, "No side conversations at the table. Bailey, you know better."

"Actually," says Donna. "It's my fault, um I um was asking where the restroom was."

"Oh dear, that's nothing to whisper, Bailey can you walk her to the restroom and wait with her." Suggests Karen.

Bailey adheres to her mother's request and guides Donna to the restroom.

It is extremely weird as Bailey literally waits near the door while Donna utilizes the restroom.

On the walk back, Donna surveys the house with her eyes. The 'weird girl' is nowhere in sight. But one thing noticed is that the house is impeccable. It is as though no one lives in it or sits on the furniture; a breathtaking view.

Not long after Donna and Tina part ways from visiting their neighbors. Tina is overly excited as she feels as though her and Karen will become great friends but Donna is still stuck on the 'weird' girl and lack of her mention.

"Mom, why do you think that the girl who welcomed us in the home wasn't at the table?" Donna questions after much thought.

"Hmm, honestly I never thought of it, I mean a blind man could see that she isn't Karen's child. Maybe she is just visiting and didn't want to congregate with everyone." Tina states without much thought.

"Mom, really? That's your explanation? Since when do you have a visitor but you don't include them in your mealtime? That's weird as fuck," smirks Donna.

Tina surprised at her daughter's language, "You watch your words and your tone young lady. I, for one enjoyed the evening. Besides, they were all so nice and polite and oh my goodness did you see the home? It was simply beautiful. It wouldn't hurt if you learned to keep house like they do, so pretty and neat."

"Anyway," smirks Donna. "I am going to the store to get me some holiday cookies and hot chocolate. All I want to do is enjoy the rest of the evening sitting in front of the television watching movies while snacking. Do you need anything?"

"Yes, I will text you my list." Says Tina happily as that means she doesn't have to take a trip to the store.

"List," Donna says while rolling her eyes. "You know what, whatever, just text it to me."

Donna leaves home and drives almost thirty minutes to the nearest store.

While inside the store she is reading her text message from her mom who texted at least eight items needed. "Geez," thought Donna. "I will be here all night."

Donna lifts her head from reading the text and to her surprise is a very nice looking tall blue-eyed blonde-haired guy standing nearby.

"Hi," says Donna, as the guy caught her staring.

"Hello," says the guy. He reaches over Donna to grab an item on the shelf near her.

He then walks away.

"Stupid, stupid, stupid." Thought Donna. "He is so dreamy and fine."

Donna proceeds to get items needed from the store. She is able to find all but one item from her mom's list.

She proceeds to the line to checkout and the dreamy guy is in front of her. Thinking she must do something quickly to get his attention, Donna pushes her basket into the back of his feet. He almost falls over.

"I am so sorry." Donna lies.

Embarrassed, the guy says, "It's okay? If you are in a hurry you can go in front of me, I am not in a rush."

"Oh," laughs Donna. "Nope, no hurry, actually I don't have anything to do, nothing at all, just passing time in a store, bored, bored, bored."

The guy chuckles then he walks up to the cashier and checks out his items. He then leaves the store.

"Well damn," thought Donna. "That didn't go very

well."

Donna purchases her items then walks out of the store.

"Hey," someone shouts.

Donna looks back and it's the dreamy guy. He apparently waited outside for her to finish her purchase.

"Hi," says Donna in a shy acting voice. "I thought you left."

"Well," says the guy. "You seemed to want my attention so here I am, you have my ear."

"Oh, um this has never happened to me before, I don't even know what to tell you." Donna says as she playfully flirts.

The two casually converse. The guy introduces himself as 'Chad'. He is a local from the area visiting family for the holidays. Chad is twenty-two years old and single. He wants to hang out and go on a date with Donna but there is one problem; his college roommate, who had nothing to do for the holidays traveled with him and he doesn't want to leave him alone. So as long as Donna has someone to go out with Chad's roommate, they can all go and hang out, sort of like a double date.

Donna, who does not know any female that can double date with her lies saying, "Sure here is my number call me later we can all four go out."

Chad and Donna both walk off to their own vehicles. Donna is smiling from ear to ear as Chad is dreamy and just the best-looking man Donna has ever laid eyes on.

Donna drives all the way back to her mother's house in a daze nearly bumping a deer; thinking about Chad.

Donna arrives at her mother's home. While unpacking the items purchased Chad calls Donna. The two speak for over two hours. Donna is ecstatic.

A few days go by; Donna and Chad have spoken everyday all day. Both are home from college with nothing to do but run up their cell phone data.

After a few days of talking Chad texts Donna, *'Tonight is the night, we can't wait to see the two of you; I can't wait to hug you.'*

Donna totally forgot that she lied about having someone for Chad's roommate.

She keeps thinking that had she not dug around trying to follow up on her last roommate maybe she would have come home with her for the holidays and all would be well. But nonetheless Donna is alone with no one to double date with her.

She opens her phone to text Chad to come clean, but she has another text message from him, '*I have enjoyed the last few days more than you know. Tonight, is the only night I can see you because I have to return back to school soon to prepare for the next semester; I can't wait to see you later.*' He adds emojis and Donna is just smitten.

Just that fast Donna forgets about the fact that she has no one to double with her. She is digging for clothes in her closet, wondering how she will wear her long brunette hair.

Her mom knocks on her room door. "Donna, dear I'm thinking pizza for dinner do you want pepperoni?"

"Oh", says Donna as she is startled by her mom. "Actually, I have a date, I was supposed to tell you a few days ago but it went by so fast."

"Of course, it goes by fast when all you do is stay on the phone 24/7. I am not blind Donna, I know there is a boy involved, so what's his name, where does he live, how old is he? Spill the beans."

Donna is now laughing hysterically. "Mom, it's not that serious, I met him at the store, we are going to hang out tonight, it'll be a double date and oh my goodness! A double date, dang, I was supposed to find his friend a date.'

"What," asks Tina confused. "Why where you finding his friend a date?"

"Mom, it's complicated, his friend is home with him and he doesn't want to leave him alone." Says Donna sarcastically.

"And that's complicated," smirks Tina. "You don't know anyone here so how are you going to bring a date for his friend? I suggest you call him and explain, we just moved here you don't know anyone. The only people you've even taken the time to meet since you have been here are the neighbors and well the twins are sixteen, there is no way they should be involved in your shenanigans."

Donna runs up to her mom and hugs her. "You are a genius mom. I am going over to the neighbors; I will be right back."

Donna runs out of the house before her mom can question or stop her.

She knocks on the door of the one neighbor nearby. The 'weird' girl opens the door.

"Perfect," mumbles Donna. "Hi, remember me? My name is Donna, I know this is short notice but would you like to come with me on a date? I mean a double date of course, me, you and two guys?"

'NO.' Says the girl firmly. As she is attempting to close the door in Donna's face, Karen walks near and inquires who is at the door.

"I am sorry to bother you, I was just asking her, well I am going on a date with a friend this evening and he has a friend and I was offering her to come along with us and just hang out." Donna says very nervously as she doesn't even know the girls' name.

Surprisingly Karen begins to smile. "That would be lovely."

Both Donna and the 'weird' girl who are standing nearby look at Karen in shock.

"Um really?" Donna asks, "She can come?"

"But of course." Karen states while smiling. "Give her ample time to prepare than come and get her. You must bring her back by midnight as that is the curfew in this house, no exceptions."

"Yes, yes ma'am I promise I will have her back by curfew." Donna excitedly says. She then leaves and rushes back home to prepare for her date.

Donna is so excited she forgot to ask the 'weird' girls' name.

Donna informs her mom what is going on, she also gives her mom details of the date as her mom is very particular about knowing her whereabouts especially in a new town.

Instead of walking, Donna drives over to pick up the girl as they are going to be driving to meet up with the guys.

Donna walks up to the home, but no one answers. Donna becomes nervous as she remembers the girl initially said no when asked if she wanted to go on the double date.

 A few moments later Karen opens the door.

"I am sorry to keep you waiting. Wanda usually opens the door but she is getting prepared, you are welcome to come inside, she will be ready shortly. It's an exciting night, one date can lead to amazing things. I told her to take her time and properly prepare herself, do come inside." says Karen in a very welcoming voice.

"Um that's ok." Says a quiet Donna. "I will wait in the car I need to input the address in my GPS."

Donna walks back to her car. Three minutes later Wanda walks out the door and enters the car.

"Hi Wanda, oh your mom? I mean Karen said your name at the door," says Donna.

"Ok." Wanda says in an unsettling tone.

Donna tries making small talk but it is useless.

Donna is now tired of the awkward silence. "So, we are going to dinner at an entertainment complex. We can eat and all get to know one another then play games and just chill. Don't worry I won't have you out past your curfew; my mom also wants me home at a decent time."

Wanda, now sitting with her arms crossed remains silent.

"So, is that your real hair?" Asks an intrigued Donna.

Wanda gives Donna a blank stare but spoke nothing in

response.

Donna is worried that Wanda will ruin the night if she acts all stinky in front of the guys.

"Look Wanda." Yells Donna. "I get it, you don't know me. You don't know the guys and you are nervous, but it's okay. It doesn't have to be this hard to socialize. Just act like you are having a good time. Nothing has to happen; jeez it's only hanging out."

Wanda remains silent.

Donna continues talking as they pull up to the destination. "How old are you, I'm 21 you look around my age and well to be honest I don't know anyone my age who doesn't like casual dating and hanging," says Donna.

"I am 33." Says Wanda, still with arms folded.

"Whoa!" Screams Donna. "You look so much younger. How do you get your skin to look so young, is there a cream that you people use? Like I would not have asked you to come had I known your age. I am in college and so are the guys, like we are all in our early 20's. Do you have a problem dating a younger man? I mean you don't have to officially date him or anything, just hang out for the night."

"I don't date, I don't hang out," says Wanda.

Donna parks the car. "Don't you want to get married one day? Have kids? I mean you kind of have to date to do that, and while you are talking how are you connected to Karen, I mean clearly you all aren't related." Says Donna.

"Our families have been connected for years." Wanda says abruptly.

"Oh ok," says Donna. "I get that, my mom has friends that she has been connected with and it's like one big family. That's pretty cool actually. Come on let's go and find the guys."

The two ladies vacate the car and enter the entertainment building. The guys are sitting in the lobby waiting area. Donna spots Chad and embraces him. Chad introduces his roommate 'Ben' while Donna introduces Wanda. Ben is just as tall as his roommate. He has red hair and freckles. He also wears glasses; he is not nearly as attractive as his 'dreamy' friend. The quartet share handshakes then await instructions to be seated for dinner.

Chad and Donna are very cozy with one another while Wanda is distant and very quiet. Ben tries to talk with Wanda but is unsuccessful.

Donna notices Wanda giving the cold shoulder so she intercepts. "Wanda, let's go to the powder room."

Wanda and Donna excuse themselves from the table and walk off to the restroom.

Donna immediately tears into Wanda. "Like really? Can you at least act normal for a second? You are acting like you have never been on a date, or in the company of a man, snap out of it and loosen up."

Wanda, with her arms folded looks Donna up and down. "Excuse you? I said *No* when you came over yet you still asked Karen, why? I am a grown woman. I told you no. Why couldn't you just leave! I don't want to be here!"

"Well, we are already here. Besides it's a forty-five-minute drive back. Can you please just loosen up. Act like you're on a date with a guy you like. I don't care, just loosen up." Says Donna very angrily.

"This is my first date." Wanda mumbles just loud enough for Donna to hear.

"I'm sorry, this is what? You are 33 years old how is that even possible? Wait that means, oh my goodness you are a virgin?!" Donna is now concerned yet somewhat confused.

"This wasn't a good idea can I use your phone to call Karen?" Asks Wanda as she has her right hand extended out for Donna's cell phone.

"You don't have your phone with you, I mean no, please just wait, please, we won't stay long, please I will never ask you to do this again. Please just stay." Begs Donna.

"Whatever," shrugs Wanda.

The two ladies walk back to the table where Chad and Ben are talking and laughing. Wanda is still awfully quiet but her hands are no longer folded together.

The two couples eat dinner then they play a few games of bowling and miniature golf. Roughly after eleven Wanda reminds Donna of her curfew. Donna does not want to leave as she and Chad are getting along perfectly, but she did promise Karen she'd have Wanda back home by midnight.

The guys are complete gentlemen. They even walk the

ladies to their car. Ben reaches out both arms for a friendly hug but Wanda isn't having it. Instead, she shakes his hand and waits for Donna from the inside of the car.

Donna on the other hand is making out with Chad. The pair is kissing and hugging so tight a mosquito couldn't fit in between them.

After a few moments, Wanda who is tired of waiting honks the horn.

The sound alarms Donna and grabs her attention. Shortly after she has entered the vehicle with Wanda.

"Tonight was magical." Donna says with a huge grin.

Wanda rolls her eyes.

The two ladies ride the entire forty-five minutes in silence.

"Boom," says Donna. "I kept my word. I brought you back with seven minutes to spare."

Wanda, who is now totally over the night exits the car without saying a word.

Donna watches her to be sure she enters safely inside

the home as they do live in the country where wild animals regularly make their presence known.

Wanda bypasses the front door and proceeds to the back of the house.

"She is so strange." Donna mumbles as she opens her car door and proceeds to peek out at Wanda to be sure she makes it safely inside her home.

Wanda bypasses the side door, instead she continues walking towards the outhouse which is the size of a small shed.

"Wanda," shouts Donna. "I can wait for you until you are ready to go inside."

Wanda turns around and yells, "Go home Donna."

Donna is now running up towards Wanda. "Look I am sorry. I didn't even thank you for coming tonight. You were a lifesaver. I only want to be sure you make it in safely, that's all. I mean no harm."

"*This* is my home." Wanda says with embarrassment.

"Oh, ok." Donna is speechless. "Um I thought well um ok so do you need me to wait until you turn the lights on?"

"I have a flashlight." Says Wanda very quietly. "I will be fine, goodnight."

"Wait," Donna says as she gently grabs Wanda's arm. "Look I don't mean to pry or anything but are you ok, like for real?!"

"I am fine. Like I said this is my home. Goodnight." Smacks Wanda.

Donna is just not understanding. Wanda is a 33-year-old woman living in an out-house with no electricity. She is a virgin and acts as though she has no sense of normalcy about her.

"Wanda what's your phone number?" Asks Donna who is trying to piece together the situation.

"What? What kind of question is that?" Responds Wanda defensively.

"You don't have a phone, do you? At the restaurant you asked to use my phone. Wanda what is going on? What grown woman doesn't have a phone?' Asks Donna in totally confusion.

"You should really go." Says Wanda who proceeds to walk towards the out-house.

Donna is now even more concerned. "Please if you are in danger can you tell me? I know I was a jerk for practically forcing you to come out tonight, I get that. But what's going on? The first time I saw you, you never really spoke and hurried away. When my mom and I came over you answered the door but was never seen again, not even to sit and visit with us, and now tonight it's like, I don't know it's just a little weird. I have never met anyone quite like you and well I don't know what to make of it. If you don't want to talk to me fine, I will just knock on the front door and tell Karen that something is going on with you and she needs to get you some form of help."

Donna turns around and runs toward the front of the house.

"I have to live here forever." Cries Wanda in tears.

Donna turns around in confusion. "What?"

Wanda, now with tears slowly streaming down her silky dark skin hesitates to talk. "My inherited last name is Friedman. My great, great grandfather was purchased by the Friedman's many years ago. The Friedman's owned the largest plantation in the bayou. Acres and large fields of cotton. Countless horses and a mansion big enough to fit the entire presidents' white house. They employed half of the police as their nighttime 'watch' security and held massive parties with the elite which included politicians and wealthy socialites. The Friedman's were the most respected well-known family in all the southern states.

When Larry Friedman Sr. died at the ripe age of 79, his legally binding will was read. In it stated that my great, great grandfather and every generation after him, belongs to the Friedman's. We are to work for them in exchange for free room and board and live on their property with no pay. We are to take care of the family when they are sick, cook their food daily, do their laundry, tend to their children upon their request, and be at their beckon call.

Karen is an heir of Larry Friedman Sr. Her mother inherited my mother and well Karen, she was gifted my mother's only child; me.

I refuse to date. I refuse to have a relationship with a man because that may lead to me birthing children. Without continuing a branch of my family tree, I am able to stop the generational curse of the Larry Friedman Sr. will."

There is a considerably awkward silence.

Prior to Donna, who is utterly stunned, having a chance to speak the outside lights from the house is turned on and a voice is near the side door.

It is Karen. "Wanda, is that you? Are you back? The twins need you. They have been invited to an elite gathering to be held tomorrow morning at the Southside Country Club; they need their clothes ironed right now."

Later that night Wanda journals her thoughts….

I am my ancestor's creation. Bought with a price that can never be repaid. Taken at once without regard to my life. All I remember seeing is the transporter sitting behind me holding a sharp well-bladed knife. In your eyes I am merely property. Something that can be purchased and sold, but what you don't know is that I have educated myself while traveling this long journey on the road. I am human my blood is red. I care. I cry. I am more than just someone who sings your spoiled infant daughter a nightly lullaby. You will respect me. You will call me by name. And as for me, I will forgive you without casting a shred of blame.

We Woke Up

Tainted Love

"Hello, this is Ethel how may I help you?" Ethel asks as she listens to the caller on the other end of her phone.

Ethel addresses the caller. "Oh my, I can't believe you are calling me, how are you? Is everything ok? Why you never call me, oh dear Lord what is it, is it… oh my, well what can I do? I need to get on a plane right now I need to," she pauses. "Well yes, I understand. Please call me back I just worry so much and I, yes, yes, I understand you are only doing your job. Thank you for calling but can you, oh my um ok thanks I will talk to you later someone is knocking on my door. I have to go."

Ethel ends the call then opens the front door; it is her friend Daisy.

Ethel to Daisy, "You will never guess who just called, I am at a loss for words I just don't…"

Daisy interrupts her friend. "Wait don't tell me yet I have been wanting to tell you about my day since earlier, girl I met the man of my dreams."

Ethel sarcastically with a smile says, "Again? Oh, I

mean really?"

"Yes, his name is Ernest." Says Daisy with a returning smirk. "And I want to invite him over for Thanksgiving. I know you cook every year and well since you and I always get together can I invite him?"

"Well, I mean you just met him and Thanksgiving is next week and well I just have so much on my mind right now and I just don't know." Gripes Ethel.

Daisy ignores her friend. "Great it's settled, we will be here bright and early on Thanksgiving. Oh, and I know you hate strangers coming over to your home so…." Daisy pulls out her cell phone and sends a text message. "You got it?" She asks Ethel.

Ethel is looking confused. "Got what?"

"Check your phone. I just sent you a picture of me and my new man so there, he is no longer a stranger and we will both be here on Thanksgiving."

Ethel looks at her phone. A text message is pending on her phone. The text message goes through and on it is a picture of a male in his mid-fifties with a big smile and a gold tooth pictured alongside Daisy.

"Oh," says Ethel. "I guess he isn't a stranger anymore."

The two ladies share a friendly laugh.

Daisy leaves soon after. Ethel sits at her kitchen table with a pen and paper. She starts to write.

She is thinking out loud while writing:

'I hope this letter finds you, I was having a bad day, a really bad day. You see my lights were almost disconnected. I recently lost hours at work due to a budget cut. I have had water damage in my home due to recent hurricanes and well I have just been so lonely. But when I received the call saying that you were missing well, I forgot all about my irrelevant needs and began to be thankful to have you in my life. You are such an amazing person and I am so proud of you. I don't know if you ever read my letters but you are the reason I keep going. You are my light in a dark room, my sunshine on a rainy day. You my dear are the reason I look to the heavens and say thank you. I love you.'

Ethel starts talking aloud while getting up from the table. "Well let me drop this off to the post office and then it's off to the store for my Thanksgiving menu."

Ethel leaves home to go on her errands.

Once she leaves the post office, she decides to go to the newly built grocery store in the city. She usually does not travel to different grocery stores as she has one near her house that she loves but the new grocery store has a huge sale on beverages. Because she is having a few people over for Thanksgiving Ethel knows she will need drinks and a few other items and there is no need spending extra money when there is a sale at this grocery store.

Ethel arrives and immediately loves the look of the new grocery store. The employees are extremely helpful and of course the layout is simply beautiful; a grocery shoppers dream. Ethel does have a hard time locating the sale items so she stops to ask for help.

"Excuse me ma'am do you work here?" Asks Ethel to a woman who looks to be dressed in uniform.

"Why yes, I do, my name is Niki and I am the assistant manager, how may I assist you?"

"Well," says Ethel, "I saw a sign saying there is a sale on soda, but I don't see any. Can you tell me which aisle I need to go to?"

The assistant manager looks around as though she is looking for someone. "Hmm, well I don't see any of the associates that are usually in that department to tell you and I know they recently moved things around, tell you what let's take a walk, I will assist you with locating the sale items. Originally the soda along with all beverages, were in one place and other sale items were placed in other areas, but the store manager recently had the team of associates strategically place all sale items together. I missed the memo as to where everything is because I had to pick my daughter up from cheer practice."

The two ladies walk through the store together. As they walk Niki starts a conversation.

"Do you have any children?"

"Yes," states Ethel. "As a matter of fact, I have a son, only one son and I love him dearly he is the apple of my eyes. He has been in the military for years and boy do I miss him. It gets lonely you know, without your child nearby."

Ethel then looks through her handbag and pulls out her wallet. "Darn, I had a picture of him but I must have forgot to replace it when I switched wallets. I just purchased this wallet. I kept my old one and wanted to transfer everything to one, I just forgot to do so."

"It's okay, no problem at all." Says a very friendly

Niki.

Niki then notices an associate and inquires of the sale items. She is informed it is near the deli as there are free samples for all store guests. Niki decides that she will continue to walk Ethel to the area, as she wants to check out the free samples.

The two ladies continue their walk through the store. Niki tells Ethel that her church is having a family and friends night. She invites Ethel as it's a good time for women to fellowship and possibly meet new people since she is missing her son.

"Oh," Niki happily says. "Let me show you a picture of my daughter, she is nine years old. My husband and I started late. It's funny because most people think she's my grandchild but nope, she is my one and only baby girl."

Niki reaches for her cell phone and on the screensaver is a picture of a beautiful little girl with Niki and a man.

The man on the photo looked incredibly familiar to Ethel.

"Oh, I am sorry, I need my glasses." Ethel places her glasses on to get a better view.

"Umm Dear." Ethel is now staring at the photo. "Who the hell is this?" She asks as she points to the guy in the photo.

"Oh, that's my husband. We have been together for fourteen years but only married for eleven. He is my soulmate; I couldn't imagine my life without him. Everything I prayed for in a man I have in him. He is so spontaneous. This year for Thanksgiving he wants us to do a late-night dinner so that we can stay up late and put up the Christmas tree for our daughter. Isn't that amazing? He is always thinking of ways to make memories. Ernest is truly one of a kind."

"*Ernest*, I thought he looked familiar, especially that gold tooth and big smile, but I was hoping I was not seeing correctly." Mumbles Ethel.

Niki stops walking. "Excuse me, how do you know my husband?"

Ethel has to think quickly as she didn't realize Niki heard her. "I um I saw him at a store and he helped me and isn't it funny I ran into him and he helped me and I ran into you and you helped me and oh shit what do you know is that the deli? Goodbye got to go!"

Ethel walks away from Niki as quickly as her legs

allow. Once far enough from her, Ethel pulls out her phone and takes another glance at the photo Daisy sent her earlier. "Well, I'll be damned." Ethel whispers under her breath.

Ethel purchases her sale items along with other groceries needed. She is contemplating how she will inform Daisy about what she just found out. Ethel and Daisy have been friends for over thirty years. The two met in college and have been inseparable ever since. They have been there through death of family members, relationships, good times, troubles; they have endured over half of their lives together. Daisy was there for the birth of Ethel's only son; her son's dad wasn't even in the room. He was held up at work and unfortunately passed away shortly after Paul Jr. was born. Daisy was there for Ethel through it all, every step of the way. Life hasn't always been easy but Daisy has been a true friend. "I just wish she knew how to pick a man." Mumbles Ethel. Daisy falls in love very easily. She was married three times and Ethel served as the matron of honor at each wedding. Daisy never had children nor did she want any. She only wanted her three ugly dogs; of course, she thinks they are precious but they are the ugliest mixed dogs ever seen with the human eyes. "Lord I just have to tell her. She is trying to bring that man to my house for Thanksgiving." Thought Ethel aloud.

Ethel leaves the grocery store then decides to call her friend while in route home. Thanksgiving is only a few days away and she doesn't want to have this news hanging over her any longer.

Ethel calls her friend and Daisy picks up the phone on the first ring.

"Hi my love," says Daisy. "What's cracking?"

Ethel takes a deep breath. "Daisy we need to talk."

"Oh, my goodness yes we do, it's like we are psychic, we are totally in-sync. We know when the other one has news." Says Daisy excitedly.

Ethel is now confused as to what her friend's news is but by the tone of her voice it must be something uplifting. Ethel decides that it would be easier for the bad news to be told first then the two friends can enjoy the good news later.

"I'm getting married." Shouts Daisy through the phone before Ethel has a chance to speak.

"*TO WHOM?*" Screams Ethel as she almost drove her

car onto the next lane.

Daisy is now laughing. "Really, you are so funny. Ernest! Ernest proposed, but before you say anything, because I know you will say it's too soon, don't worry he doesn't want to rush it. He wants us to remain engaged for at least three years so that we can take our time and plan the wedding of our dreams."

Ethel is now parked on the side of the road. Her friend is so excited and the last thing Ethel wants to do is hurt Daisy but she wouldn't be a real friend if she didn't be open and honest.

Here goes thought Ethel. "He's married Daisy. Ernest is married."

There is a moment of silence then laughter from Daisy. "Um have you been drinking Ethel? I said I am getting married!"

"Daisy please, please listen to me. I met her. He has a wife and a young daughter. His wife works at the new grocery store recently built and they have been together for many years. They are planning Thanksgiving night together since clearly, he already made day plans with you. Oh, Daisy I am so sorry to be the one to have to tell you this dear but everything happens for a reason and had I not gone to the new grocery store and met her you would be caught up in an entanglement and you are too good of a person for that. I am sorry, I really am but we will still have a great Thanksgiving as we always do and you will be sent the man of your dreams one day. I am sure that the right man will come along, you just wait and see. You are a strong Christian woman who lives a life pleasingly; everything will be fine."

Ethel knew this wasn't news her friend wanted to hear but they have been through far worse through the years.

"So, what time should Ernest and I be at your home on Thanksgiving?" Questions Daisy.

Surely Ethel is hearing her friend incorrectly. "Excuse me?!"

"Look Ethel, I know. I know he has a wife and daughter. I am ok with it. Life is short. He's happy, I'm happy so hey let's all be happy and enjoy." Daisy states very firmly.

Ethel is shocked. This is not like Daisy. She has never stayed with a man affiliated with another woman let alone date a married man.

"What the hell did he do to you Daisy? This is not you.

This is not the woman that I know you to be, what is going on? I thought the two of you just met not long ago and already you are engaged and he's married and…." Ethel is quickly interrupted by Daisy.

"Ethel! Stop it! Look I have to go. Ernest and I will be over around eleven on Thanksgiving. Goodbye."

Daisy hangs up the phone as Ethel sits in her car in a state of shock.

Ethel, after sitting in her car for over thirty minutes speechless, later returns home and cleans her house. The next few days are rather quiet; especially since she and her only friend Daisy aren't speaking. Ethel is still cleaning her home from recent devastation from hurricanes so she doesn't have much time for anyone. In fact, she doesn't even know if she'll have anyone over on Thanksgiving Day. Paul Jr. is away and Daisy isn't speaking to her; everything is just a mess.

On Thanksgiving, Ethel is still not feeling her best as the last few days have been long and tiresome, but one thing she never misses is a chance to host Thanksgiving at her home even if she's all alone.

Ethel prepares her thanksgiving meal. Shortly after there is a knock on the door. Ethel opens the door and it is her friend Daisy along with Ernest. Ethel greets the two and introduces herself to Ernest.

"Well, hello I am Ethel." She leans forward and extends her hand.

"Hello, very nice to meet you I am Ernest." He says with a large grin.

"Of course, do come in. I just finished putting the last of the side dishes on the table, please grab a seat." Ethel states while rolling her eyes at Daisy.

Daisy ignores her friends' eye roll and excitedly says, "Ethel girl I have so much to tell you. Me and Ernest have spent every day together and well it has been amazing. We went shopping and to the movies a few cities away, and we even went visit his mother. Can you believe it? It has been so amazing." Daisy then notices her friend isn't paying attention and looks somewhat distracted. "Ethel what is wrong? Do you hear me why are you looking so down? It's thanksgiving and well perk up, what's wrong…"

Ethel, looks very unattached. "Well, I wasn't going to say anything, but I am just so heartbroken. I have been trying to hold it all in but I can't take it anymore. I received a call from the Army Sargent and well, Paul

Jr's army aircraft went missing about a week ago".

Daisy is in shock. "What, why didn't you tell me?"

Ethel is now in tears. "I didn't want to worry anyone and I keep writing him as I always have every week and I have been trying to reach him but no luck. I just don't know what to do."

Daisy walks close to her friend and hugs her as tight as she can.

Ernest is now feeling somewhat uncomfortable and wants to help. "Listen we don't have to stay here. There is a local army base not far from here. We can go and see if they have any information. Someone has to know something."

Daisy shakes her head in agreement. "I agree. Ethel lets go. It's no sense in staying inside. You are the one person I can always count on when I am down. You are the one that lifts me up so let me do something to help you. We will find him. I won't let you go through this alone. You have helped me in more ways than one. You have been my prayer warrior, my right hand, I love you like a sister. It's only right I am here for you."

Ethel is in tears. "Thank you, thank you both. It's time

that I stop crying and try to stay positive. Let me get my coat and we can go."

Within seconds there is a quick knock and in walks Ethels' son, Paul Jr.

"Momma!" Yells Paul Jr.

Daisy, Ernest, and Ethel all are overwhelmed with joy. Ethel runs toward her son and the two embrace one another.

Paul Jr. removes his hat while speaking. "It's so good to be home, thank you mother it is because of you that I am here."

Ethel is standing near her son and though happy to see him she looks awfully confused.

Paul Jr. while still embracing his mother says, "Your letters, your letters have kept me for the last two years. Your letters of hope and encouragement has kept me going when I didn't want to go on any longer. When we went missing many lost all hope. But I held on because of the letters I read. I remember you telling me, 'life doesn't stop until you do' and 'be unstoppable in all you do.' Thank you for inspiring me in ways you will never know. Words may not mean much to some but just a few words of encouragement each day allowed me to be better than the days before. When the emergency chopper found us stuck on a deserted land, I wanted to find a way to call you but when I returned to the army grounds waiting was a new letter from you, and I knew that you had been praying for me and thinking of me, so I sought approval and jumped on the first flight here. Thank you for inspiring me, thank you for not giving up on me. Thank you for taking time to encourage me; thank you, thank you, thank you. I know life hasn't always been easy for you and you have your bad days just as anyone else but you don't understand the power of words and how essential words are to people around you. Words live on beyond the tone of your voice, further than the words on paper. Words can haunt you or it can help you. Thank you for allowing your words to always be positive…now let's eat."

Paul Jr. proceeds to walk toward the dinner table then looks at Ernest. "Who the hell are you?"

Ernest laughs. "I am Ernest. I'm a *friend* of Daisy's."

"*A friend?* He is so funny, He's actually my fiancé." Says Daisy as she shows off her engagement ring.

"Congratulations," says Paul Jr. "Let me know ahead of time so that I can arrange to be home for the wedding."

He looks over at his mom. "So, matron of honor for the fourth time huh mom?"

He then laughs but notices his mom does not look happy.

"Oook," mumbles Paul Jr. "Um, so can we eat now or is anyone else coming over?"

"Well, that depends on Ernest." Says Ethel with her hands folded across her chest.

Now everyone is looking confused.

Ethel continues to speak and looks directly at Ernest. "Is Niki joining us or is she at home with your daughter?"

"YOU ARE OUT OF LINE ETHEL!" Screams Daisy from the top of her lungs.

"He introduced you as his *friend.* This man is not going to marry you in three years or thirty years. I have seen his wife. I saw a picture of him with his family. He is using you Daisy. Don't be that woman. Don't be the woman that breaks up a happy home." Says Ethel as she tries to embrace Daisy.

Paul Jr. and Ernest stand still not saying anything. Paul

Jr. doesn't fully understand what is going on.

Daisy rejects Ethels embrace. "*If* the home was happy, he would not be here with me. This is my life Ethel. My life; my decisions. Who are you to dictate the way I live my life? Your loyalty is to me not some lady at a grocery store. Can you please be happy for me? Look at me! I wasn't blessed with a nice skin tone. My nose is so wide I can fit large marbles up my nostrils. My body isn't in tip top shape. My stomach sits further out than my ass, and well I don't really have men banging down my door trying to get with me. I am charcoal black with hair as nappy as carpet, far from '*America's standard of beautiful.*' Daisy turns away and says sternly to Ernest. "Come on bae we are leaving."

"Wait," cries Ethel. "Daisy you are my sister. Not by blood but through love. We have lived our entire adult lives together. Daisy, I simply want what's best for you. I know you are still hurting because Karen broke up your marriage and stole your husband but you have to let that hurt go! It will eat away at you. You are such an amazing woman; a God-fearing woman. I see you on the weekends leading the woman's empowerment groups and speaking life to your sister circle. Daisy you can't love just the women in your 'circle.' You can't! You must have an open heart. Ernest's wife is a sister!

She is another black woman who has done nothing wrong to you, yet you knowingly hurt her to make yourself feel better. Don't be that woman. Don't be the woman who willingly hurts another. Be the woman that other women can look up to. Be the woman that inspires for greatness. You can't pick and choose which 'sister' should be respected. *WE* all deserve respect. I get it, Lord knows I do. Black men are beautiful creatures and it gets lonely at times but we have too many people fighting us, for us to purposely hurt one another. I know you are still hurt by the fact that many moons ago your man was stolen by Karen. Yes, it was wrong for that woman to come in and steal your man while pretending to be your friend. But Karen was an over privileged, floozy who thought her shit didn't stink because of the blue-eyed family she was born into. Please, I beg you; do better, be better. Don't stoop to the level of which you have grown simply because of past hurt. We, black women, have come too far as a people to just lay down, accept anything that comes our way, and forget that we too are born of queens."

Daisy stares at Ethel but utters nothing.

After a split-second Daisy grabs Ernest's right hand and the two leave abruptly.

Ethel is left standing in her living room unable to fight
back tears.

Time passes. Paul Jr. has returned to his base but
remains in contact with his mother.

 Daisy is still 'engaged' to Ernest.

Ernest is still married to Niki.

Three years have gone by.

Ernest has not divorced his wife nor has he made
concrete plans to marry Daisy.

Ethel and Daisy have not spoken since that
Thanksgiving Day.

Ethel journals her thoughts....

Things are not always what they seem. The pictures are lovely. The smiles oh so sweet but when you look a little deeper what do you see? Is it truly happiness? Do the pictures tell the truth or is it that you are defeated but afraid to embrace life as it is? You go to parties happy as can be but when you look in the mirror what exactly do you see? Take off the mask, look beyond the surface, and be true to yourself. Are you really content or is it that you merely settled with what you think is heaven sent? God will not send what does not belong, carefully think about all your wrongs. Is this what you want? Is it truly worth it? Or do you need time to look in the mirror and be reminded that your crown still fits.

We Woke Up

My Crown, My Choice

"This makes absolutely no sense. I have been steadily employed since I graduated college and just like that, I have no job? Ugh I hate this new merger it is ridiculous; no one stood a chance. They literally fired my whole team without notice! Wait mom I have an incoming call, it's Dave, my boyfriend I will talk to you later, love you." Michelle says as she hurries to end the call so she can speak with her boyfriend.

"Dave," screams Michelle. "I miss you so much when are you returning from your business trip? I have so much to tell you."

Dave, while blowing kisses through the phone says, "I will be home soon enough my dear. I had a few moments in between my presentation and well I just wanted to check on my favorite girl."

Michelle is blushing. "You always make me smile. Just hearing your voice made me forget all of my troubles. This week has been so very stressful. The company finally finished their merger and well as anticipated I lost my job. Ten years of hard work and just like that I am out searching for a new career. This sucks! They didn't even give any of us the opportunity to apply for any of the open positions, just handed us walking papers and they expect us to move on. It hurts. I mean, I get it, it's only a job but I loved what I did and more importantly I was good at it. On the bright side I do have two weeks of severance pay so I guess I can relax and unwind; for two weeks anyway."

"Babe don't worry you will land on your feet. There is something better waiting for you, something even better than what you lost. Air hug my love. I have to get back to work but I will call you later." Dave ends the call making kissing noises.

Michelle hangs up and notices the time. She rushes out and drives to a nearby coffee house. She along with her co-workers agreed to meet up to 'job hunt' together. Her team consisted of her and four others. All hard workers who were distraught about the changes that occurred at their employment.

Michelle arrives at the coffee house but sees no one she recognizes.

"Hmm, must be early." She mumbles. Michelle then orders a blueberry mocha along with a danish muffin and decides to enjoy a snack while waiting for the others to arrive.

Ten minutes passes by yet no one shows up. Michelle is certain that she is at the correct address and even more certain of the meet up time yet no one arrived to greet her.

After an additional twenty minutes of waiting Michelle contacts Karen, an associate from her team who she considers a friend.

The phone rings but Karen does not answer. Michelle leaves a voicemail. She then proceeds to call another associate when Karen returns her call.

Michelle answers the phone quickly. "Karen? Where are you? Surely, I have misinformation about the meet up, no one is here. Did you all decide to meet at another location or did something change? What is…"

Michelle is abruptly interrupted by Karen who says, "Michelle I can get in trouble for talking to you. We were instructed by human resources to not speak to anyone no longer working for the company."

Now confused, Michelle asks, "What? What are you speaking of?"

Karen takes a deep breath and pauses. "We didn't get fired, only you."

Michelle is taken back as she is utterly lost. "What are you talking about? I read all of the memos, was at all of the mandatory meetings and have been very involved in the merger since we were all first informed. It was clear that *we* were all getting fired. We even met after some of the corporate meetings to strategize how we'd handle the transition. We all decided that we would meet here, at the coffee shop to vent and begin searching for new jobs."

"We decided that prior to going in the office with the new boss," smirks Karen. "But once we separately went in, we were each praised for the work we do and well after that meeting, we all had a quick 'meet and greet' with the new employees and supervisors. I wanted to call you but well, I heard that you were fired so I didn't know how to talk with you plus we were advised to not speak to anyone no longer affiliated with the company. But don't worry I know you will find another job; you were one of the best employees. I mean you actually trained me and well you have the education and experience; you will be fine. I am confident that all will work out well for you."

Michelle is mixed with emotions. She doesn't know if she wants to cry, scream, or turn over the tables in front of her.

"Look I wish you the best, bye." Karen ends the call prior to Michelle having a chance to speak.

Michelle gathers herself then leaves the coffee shop. She is understandably upset and unable to begin looking for employment.

When she returns home there is a notice on her door that reads:

'3B TENANT YOU HAVE 15 DAYS TO VACATE THE PREMISES. ON THE 16TH DAY THE LOCKS WILL BE CHANGED AND YOU WILL NOT BE ALLOWED RE-ENTRY INTO THE BUILDING.'

She pulls the note off her door. "Surely they have the wrong apartment." She states under her breath while ripping the notice.

Michelle enters her apartment, pours herself a glass of her favorite wine, and drinks until she falls asleep on the sofa.

A few days pass by and Michelle has still not found the courage to restart the transition for a new job. She has fallen into a slight depression and keeps replaying the call with Karen. The fact that Karen, who was tardy for work more than anyone in the company and never finished her work on time was offered to stay makes no sense.

By the eighth day Michelle pulls herself out of her funk. She is highly pissed that not one of her co-workers reached out to her and has ill feelings about her predicament but life has to continue.

She applies for over ten jobs with advertisements in the local paper. By day twelve she finally receives an email requesting an interview. She is out of touch with the interview process as she has not had to do one in years but she nails it. Only problem is she wasn't immediately offered the job, which means now the waiting game begins.

Michelle tries to keep herself occupied over the next few days. Between talking on the phone with her boyfriend and drinking wine she applies for additional jobs in hopes one will hire her. While she is at home one evening, with a belly filled with wine there is a loud knock on the door.

Not expecting anyone she is utterly surprised. She opens the door only to find two men dressed in police uniform at the door with her landlord.

"Today is the 16th day; get out." The landlord firmly

states.

Michelle is taken back by this. "You must have the wrong apartment. I have paid my rent on time every month since moving here."

She proceeds to close the door but the officer stops the closure with his foot.

The officer looks Michelle directly in the eyes and says, "Ma'am you need to vacate the building."

She walks away from the door leaving the two police officers and landlord standing in the doorway. She walks to her bedroom where she maintains her receipts. Within a few moments she is able to show the landlord and police receipts of rent payment from the past year; she has never skipped a payment.

"Ma'am," states the landlord, "I see this and it looks like you submitted everything online which is our process but we have no record of your rent payments." The landlord then takes a closer look. "Do you see this?" He asks. "Look, there is a difference in your receipt from the past two months versus prior months; did you do something differently because this is not our generated receipts, we do not have these last two payments."

Michelle, along with the officers take a closer look. The landlord is correct. There is an oddly noticeable difference between the receipts.

"I did everything t-the same." Michelle says as she stutters with nervousness. "Nothing was different on my part, when you upgraded your system and sent the new links, I followed it precisely. I had no trouble logging in or paying."

"What? What do you speak of?" Asks the Landlord. "I have never 'upgraded' my system?!"

She is now staring at the landlord. The police are standing in confusion. "Yes, yes you did, you sent me an email with new links and I followed it and I paid and you sent these receipts."

The police look at one another before one begins to speak. "Ma'am it appears that you may have been cyber swindled. Someone sent you over information in an attempt to hack you and well, instead of you paying your rent you seemingly paid them."

They are all now standing in silence for a moment.

One of the officers look at the landlord. "Look I can't tell you what to do but considering the circumstances you may want to give her some time to look into this matter." The officer turns to Michelle. "Ma'am you have the right to file an official police report at this time."

"*YES*," shouts Michelle. "Please I want to. I mean I am just not understanding any of this."

"May I ask you somewhat of a ridiculous question?" Asks one of the officers to Michelle. "Has anyone been in your home? Witnessed these receipts? Or have you had any alerts of security breaches? Someone has to have known how the correct receipts looked in an effort to duplicate it and email you the new links to pay your rent."

"No." Michelle states while shaking her head. "I hardly have any visitors; no one knows where I keep my receipts. My boyfriend may be able to help, he's tech savvy. I can call him, hang on…."

Michelle's attempt to contact her boyfriend is unsuccessful.

The landlord agrees to give her fifteen additional days to figure out what is going on but he is addiment about wanting to collect the rent. The police take Michelle's written statement before leaving.

Michelle pours herself another glass of wine. She tries calling her boyfriend again to tell him of her day but he doesn't respond.

Michelle goes back on her phone and realizes that she hadn't talked to her boyfriend on the day before either; oddly he hadn't called or texted even though he was consistent with communication since they began dating three months ago.

She decides to text him: *babe call me ASAP, like seriously I need your help. CALL ME.*

Michelle waits but doesn't get a response. She falls asleep on the sofa when she is suddenly awakened by the sounds of her phone ringing. Hoping it's her boyfriend she answers in a hurry.

"Hello, this call is for Michelle. I apologize of the late time but we are conducting interviews on tomorrow at 9:30am and we are very interested in speaking with you. Are you available to meet?" Asks the articulate caller.

"Yes I am." Michelle says with enthusiasm.

The caller gives Michelle all of the needed details.

Michelle is relieved to finally have started getting

consistent call backs from employers. "It's not a job offer but it's a start." Smirks Michelle once she hangs up.

The next morning Michelle prepares for her day. She takes extra time styling her hair. She evenly distributes her braids to one side of her head leaving the shaved side of her head noticeable to show off her new dangling earrings. She irons her clothes, shines her high heels, and then applies make-up to her face; after all she wants to make a great first impression.

Once prepared she looks up the address for the interview. After googling the address, she discovers it is near a smoothie shop that she loves.

"Not that I need a sweet treat with my big hips but I am sure going to enjoy it." Thought Michelle as she laughs out loud.

She left a few moments early to ensure she would have enough time to get her favorite smoothie; strawberry cheesecake with added peanut butter. Traffic was heavy which gave Michelle anxiety and though she didn't want to be late, she already had a taste in her mouth for the smoothie. She took a few shortcuts and was able to still make it for her snack. Upon arriving to the smoothie shop she waits over ten minutes in the drive thru line. Frightened she'll be late for her interview she decides to park and go inside rather than wait in the slow-moving drive thru line.

Michelle walks up to the counter and orders her smoothie. While waiting for her order she walks over to the left side to pick up napkins and a sipping straw when she notices Karen near a sink sanitizing her hands with two smoothies nearby.

Michelle froze for a moment, unsure if she wants to even speak with Karen considering the way she hung up on her during their last conversation. Against better judgement Michelle realizes that she was not the problem and though she and Karen no longer work together it doesn't mean they can't still be cordial to one another in public.

Michelle walks up to Karen and it is as though Karen has witnessed a ghost sighting.

"Well, aren't you at least going to say hello?" Michelle asks in a somewhat pleasant tone.

"Um well I um," Karen muffles. "Hi, um you know what I am late, I can't really talk so I am just going to leave, but um nice seeing you."

Karen grabs her smoothies and attempts walking away. She nearly runs out of the smoothie shop.

Michelle runs behind her. "Karen, wait please stop I only wanted to say hello, I just…."

Michelle stops at once. She is certain her eyes are deceiving her. Surely Michelle is not seeing this, no it can't be. Karen was actually a friend prior to everything changing at their job.

Karen is now getting in the car with a man but not just any man; she is opening Dave's car door.

"WHAT THE HELL!" Shouts Michelle as she runs near the car door prior to Karen closing it.

Michelle refuses to let go of the car door. She grabs it with all her force. Michelle makes such a scene that Dave exits the car to try and get her to calm down.

"Get away from me." Yells Michelle to her boyfriend Dave. "You, you are not supposed to be here. What are you doing? I have been calling and texting non-stop! Why are you here? With her?"

"Calm down Michelle," Dave says peacefully. "Look I am so sorry you had to find out this way but yes Karen and I are a couple. We have been since before she began working with you. Michelle you are a good woman, you really are and I actually enjoyed a few of our conversations but it was never supposed to get serious. I mean you were only someone that was in the middle of a plan. Look I don't have time for the specifics but Karen told me about the woman who trained her, a woman she described as 'perfect'. She told me how she wanted to get back at you for always being a goody two shoes at work and hogging all the spotlight in the office so…."

Karen interrupts, "So nothing. We owe her no explanation. Get in the car now; let's go Dave."

"Hello, is this 911? I need an officer to meet me at the smoothie shop on the corner of St. Bagelis street. I am about to kill this bitch and her boyfriend." Michelle says to the 911 operator as she holds her phone in her left hand and tightens her right fist.

Karen is laughing uncontrollably. "You called 911 because my boyfriend befriended you? You are hilarious."

"No, I am calling them because you two used me, and well," Michelle stops for a second then hangs up the phone with the 911 operator. "You know what, you two aren't even worth it."

Michelle looks at Dave. "Did you hack into my computer?"

Dave glances away.

"I'll take that as a yes! Wow you two deserve one another. And to think, they actually kept you and let me go at work; wow."

Michelle begins to walk away.

After a few steps she turns around. "I just want to know one thing. Just one and I promise I will never bother the two of you again."

Michelle with tears in her eyes looks at Karen. "Why, why did they keep you? I mean I get it the other team members are Christians and they take religion seriously and the new owners are well known Christens and well I can see how they may have bonded, but you? You aren't a Christian, you don't 'hang' with them nor do you speak their language. Why did they keep you? An employee who was the last to be hired. Someone who is tardy daily and I mean let's just keep it real you don't even have a good rapport with any of the team members. It makes no sense."

Karen with a devilish smile looks Michelle up and

down before saying, "Look at the way you carry yourself Michelle. You dress well, there are no complaints there. But there is more to a good employee than dressing well and doing everything asked of them. I mean seriously look at you and look at me. I am the total package and you, well just look at your hair."

Karen rolls her eyes then enters the car where Dave is now inside waiting. The two drive off.

Michelle returns to her car and journals her thoughts....

Representation Matters. Long, short, relaxed, straight, dreads, blown out, natural, fade, bald, textured, dyed, braided, gray, black, red or white it's my hair and I have my rights. This isn't up for discussion. It shouldn't even matter what I choose or how I wear it is not a debate. So, thread wisely before you attempt to relate. My hair is part of who I am and I will wear it proud. In fact, I am not scared nor ever taught to be shy. I will scream from the rooftop; I am black and I'm proud. Do me a favor just one thing I ask, when you see my hair there is no need to try to put me down, for this is my glory, my roots; my crown.

We Woke Up

You're Standing too Close

"Mom can you please let me know if it's cold out, I need to know how to dress." Shouts Salli as she looks aimlessly in her closet.

"Salli," shouts back her mom Karen, "Just put something warm on dear we are going to be late."

Salli and her mom Karen gather their things and rush out the front door. They run nearly two blocks down the street with signs in each of their hands.

Over 200 people are gathered all with signs. Police officers are standing near a group of national security men and women dressed in uniform. A police officer begins speaking on a wireless microphone:

"Stand back at once, this area is restricted. Go home. You do not belong here. I repeat this area is restricted. You will not protest on these streets. Return to your own neighborhoods."

Karen is listening to the police when she glances and witnesses her daughter running towards the crowd of petitioners trying to enter.

"Salli come back." Karen then proceeds to run towards

her daughter. An armed officer sees what is going on and races towards Salli and grabs her. Karen, now out of breath, is drawing near her daughter and the officer.

"Thank you, officer, thank you very much. Salli what is wrong with you? Why in the world would you try to run near those hoodlums?"

"Really mom? Are you serious right now? Like this is crazy. They only want to be heard and I for one think we need to go over and try to talk to them and see why they are protesting. I mean they seem harmless and…"

"Harmless? Salli you are so naïve. Those people are crooks and they are dangerous. They don't respect the law nor do they believe in justice. All they want is to create division and strive amongst us. I brought you here to stand with me and our neighbors as we protect our neighborhood. This is our town! Not theirs." Karen rolls her eyes in disgust at her daughter, grabs her, and proceeds to walk back to where they were originally standing.

Within moments there are screams heard, people are now running. Karen notices that the protesters somehow made it inside the neighborhood. A neighborhood that is restricted, overpriced, and protected by the police. Karen reaches to take her daughter by the hand but instead Salli runs in the opposite direction. Salli runs into the crowd of protestors. Karen attempts to go after her but is blinded by tear gas; tear gas that the police released to dismantle the crowd. Karen can't see and she is coughing uncontrollably. As Karen tries to navigate through the crowd she is pushed as everyone is trying to run to safety. Karen is accidentally knocked down. Because of the large amount of people in such a close proximity no one notices she is on the ground. Karen is stumbled on, kicked accidently, and unable to be heard yelling for help. Within minutes she passes out.

Karen is later seen by a protestor. He tries to help her but is unable. He runs to find help. He has trouble as tear gas is still being sprayed and the sun is now setting. Over ten minutes have passed and Karen is still on the ground, now fully unconscious. The protestor, determined to help this woman lying on the ground continues to look for help. He later sees a go-kart that may have belonged to the police. He notices keys inside. He starts the go-kart and proceeds to navigate his way back. It is difficult as his eyes are burning and darkness is steadily approaching. Several minutes later he sees Karen. He proceeds to lift her up and places her onto the go-kart. He hopes he can release her to the care of the paramedics or police but he is unsuccessful. The police have scattered and there is no first responder in sight. Fearful she may die the protester drives the go-kart out of the neighborhood and onto local traffic. As he is proceeding, he is searching for his phone but can't find it. Shortly after he remembers he gave it to his friend to videotape the protest. The protester doesn't have his cell phone, nor did he drive to the event so he doesn't have faster transportation to get Karen the help she desperately needs. He is driving as fast as he can through traffic but the go-kart does not travel top speed.

In what seems like hours, the protestor arrives at a nearby hospital. He parks near the emergency area and brings Karen inside. He doesn't know her name, address, family, or anything. All he knows is that she needs immediate medical attention. He gives a complete statement at the hospital as they rush to aide her. He is allowed to use a hospital telephone to contact his friend to inform him of his whereabouts.

Within minutes his friend arrives at the hospital to pick him up. The protestor asks the hospital if the woman will be ok, but they don't have any update. He leaves his information in case anything is needed. He then leaves with his friend.

The hospital administration does the needed work to find out who the woman (Karen) is while the doctors work to revive her.

Her identity is discovered very quickly as Karen is a nurse at the hospital. Her co-workers recognize her and they are able to contact family. Karen's sister is called. Karen's sister 'Jessie' arrives to the hospital as soon as she can. She has Salli with her as she contacted Salli soon as the hospital informed her of Karen's whereabouts.

Jessie and Salli are informed of the incident and reassured that Karen will be fine, but because she has a concussion, along with fractured ribs she will have to remain in the hospital. Jessie and Salli are relieved that Karen is expected to make a full recovery.

The two are allowed to visit Karen. Karen is bruised badly and doesn't remember anything after the fall.

"I am so sorry mom." Salli says in tears. "I never met for any of this to happen. I just wanted to go and be on the right side of things. I just wanted to help the protestors, they just want justice and oh mom, I am truly sorry."

Karen reaches out and squeezes her daughter's hand.

Jessi walks up to the other side of her sisters' bed and says, "Tell you gals what, let's forget about tonight for now and just be thankful that we are together."

Within a few days Karen is released from the hospital. She is visited by the police shortly after to follow up on her case. She informs the police she wouldn't be of much help as she doesn't remember anything after falling.

The police officer informs her, she may not be of help but he can be. The police officer proceeds by saying, "Someone saved your life. It was someone near you, possibly from your neighborhood as they were close enough to see you were in trouble. He risked his life for you. He saw you unconscious, tried to get help and was unsuccessful so he stole a go-kart, drove the kart all the way to the hospital, made sure you were safe, then gave a full statement while at the hospital. I am not sure you would have survived had it not been for him. I am here to give you his information. If you choose to use it, it's your choice, as I am sure he would be happy to hear that you are fine. Again, it's your choice whether or not you call him. He inquired about your well-being when he brought you in but because of confidentially we couldn't share any information with him. I am glad you are doing well ma'am. Take care."

The police officer leaves Karen's home.

Karen sits down and looks at the phone number. She reaches for her phone to contact the person to say thank you then realizes that her life was spared. She decides before calling that it may be better to purchase a thank you basket or small gift as a token of her gratitude.

A few minutes later Salli returns home. She was at school and had to stay late due to her junior class being assigned to lead the high school play.

"Hi mom." Says Salli as she enters the home.

"Salli, hello, how was your day?" Asks Karen.

Salli proceeds to tell her mom about the project she is working on and how she is hungry because she missed lunch due to helping her classmates with the project. She then goes on to say she couldn't even get a snack at concession because the project ended too late.

"Oh, my goodness, my poor baby." Karen says with care. "How about I make your favorite dinner? In fact, I can invite the person who saved my life to dinner. The police came and gave me their contact; this would be great. A homemade dinner to say thank you would definitely be a nice touch. Are you up for company dear? We don't have to host the person long, just enough time for them to eat and for me to say thank you. After all they saved my life that night. Lord I still can't believe those colored people pushed their way through and made it in the neighborhood. I have worked too hard and make too much money to be alongside common thugs."

"*MOM*," shouts Salli. "Are you serious, 'thugs' wow who are you?"

"Salli, I am your mother!" Karen sternly states. "I have done everything I can to protect us from the likes of those people. People who had the same opportunities as everyone else but they keep focusing on the fact that they were once slaves and are owed forty acres and a damn mule. I am so sick of them and their mentality. The nerve of them to think because they are not happy with decisions made from the judicial system that they can protest and all of a sudden life will miraculously change, they are pathetic. They need to go out and find themselves work instead of playing in the streets. Nothing is going to work in their favor. The laws are not changing for them. They need to deal with it or move back to where their ancestors came from; simply pathetic. And to think you were actually running towards them?! For what? Why? What in the world were you thinking Salli?”

“I was thinking that they need people on their side who will listen to them. The world is not fair. They were protesting because they are tired of seeing people who look like them being killed. They are exhausted seeing police cause harm then blame them for it. They are confused as to why the judicial system only works for one race and not the other. You are a nurse at a hospital mother, you of all people should have some empathy. I tried to go over to let them know they are not alone. I am sixteen and I see the world for what it is. I see how unfair laws are and how you have to be from a certain family or upbringing to get a fair chance. I see my classmates get passed up when they try out for academic groups even though they are more than qualified and meet all the guidelines. I see people look only at the surface but never what’s beneath it. I see plenty mother. I see people who were never given a fair chance expected to just deal with it and that’s not ok! It never was and it never will be. I see…”

Salli is interrupted by Karen.

“I SEE MY DAUGHTER SETTING THE TABLE FOR DINNER!”

Salli, who is in tears adheres to her mother’s directives

and she walks to the kitchen to wash her hands and prepare the dinner table.

Karen locates the phone number of the person who saved her life. She calls and identifies herself. She invites him over to dinner as her way of saying thank you. He informs her that he is overwhelmed with joy to learn that she is doing fine. He accepts the dinner invitation and is given the address to her home.

Within a few hours, Karen has prepared dinner. Stuffed roast with string beans, loaded bell peppers, dinner roll, and a red velvet two-layer cake filled with strawberries. She wants to be sure to show appreciation to the person who saved her life so she goes into her wine cabinet and takes out a bottle of her best wine. She does not intend to entertain her guest long as she has work in the morning, however she definitely wants him to feel welcomed in her home.

"Dinner looks so good mom. I can't wait to eat, I am starving." Says Salli who has not eaten all day.

"Thanks, dear, our guest will be here soon. Remember to mind your manners and I do not want you to speak of the protest or your views. Eat then remove yourself from the table immediately thereafter. Understood?"

Salli gives her mother a sarcastic look. "Yes mom, I understand."

The doorbell rings moments later. Karen opens the door and immediately, her bright smile showing all of her pearly white teeth, is now a frown.

"Hello Karen? My name is Michael, we spoke on the phone. Thank you for inviting me to your home for dinner." Michael stretches his hand out for a handshake to greet Karen.

Karen looks Michael up and down. He is a male wearing black dress shoes, khaki pants, a white shirt, and glasses. He is an African American man.

Salli rushes over to the door. She sees Michael and starts smiling from ear to ear. "Hello I'm Salli nice to meet you."

Salli attempts to shake the hand of Michael as his hand is still extended from trying to greet Karen.

Karen removes Salli's hand before it touches Michaels' hand.

"Salli, dear go inside." Karen says under her breath.

Salli looks at her mom as she doesn't understand why

her mother is pushing her away from greeting their guest. Before she could say anything her mom gently shoves her back inside their home.

"Michael Right?" Asks Karen. "I think there has been some sort of misunderstanding. Are you certain that you were the one that transported me to the hospital? Oh, and just so you know I have spoken to the police so don't think you can just show up to my home with ill intentions and get away with whatever you have planted in your mind. I know it was someone in my neighborhood as the person was near me, close enough to see me and provide help."

Michael, now withdrawing his hand from attempting to greet Karen responds. "Yes, I am certain. In fact, I have it on video. You see my friend was videotaping the protest with my phone. I was one of the first protesters inside so I had a head start. Once inside tear gas was released so I turned around because if the police were tear gassing us there was no way to be sure that they wouldn't shoot us. I turned around and saw you. I tried with all my might to help you but couldn't. I then found the go-kart, placed you on it and when I couldn't find a first responder, I drove you to the hospital. I gave a copy of my ID along with a witness statement to the police and left my telephone number. You needed help, so I help you."

Karen, looking at Michael in disgust. "Are you saying that *YOU* saved my life?"

"Yes, yes ma'am. You needed help; I was taught that when a person needs help you help them. That is what any warm-blooded human being should do; provide help. We never know when we will be in need and we may even be entertaining an angel so it's imperative that we show kindness to everyone placed in our path. I was only protesting because my people want the same help. We want help when we can't help ourselves. Help when we are sick, help when we need jobs, help when we are in trouble at no fault to our own. We want help from the judicial system that is seemingly broken. Help when we see our brothers and sisters getting pre-judged simply because of the color of their skin tone. We want help to live a life free from harassment, judgement, and bias behavior so I try my very best to help others who are in need of the same help that my people long for." Says Michael.

The two momentarily stand in silence.

"*You* saved *my* life?" Asks a confused Karen.

"Yes, I did." Replies Michael.

Karen looks Michael directly in the eyes, pauses for a split second then says in a wicked voice, "You should have let me die."

Karen closes her front door, locks it, and proceeds inside to eat dinner with her daughter!

Michael leaves and later journals his thoughts….

Why do you hate me? You look at me and stare, like I'm something you've never seen. I become uncomfortable but not for me; for you. You have no idea what it is you see. I am a child of the highest, a true work of art. I am not your average 'joe' I am articulate and smart. I am a father, brother, uncle, and son. You never gave me a chance because it was easier to judge. Never tried to get to know me or see life through my eyes. You don't care if I have principles or question my views on life, instead you see me and your mind goes back to when I was sold for a price. I am no longer that person, they died long ago. I am someone who you should take the time to know. I have grown into a person with feelings as deep as the sea, yet my question remains, why do you hate me?

We Woke Up

If Not You Then Who

"Lenard do you really have to leave? It's the weekend. Why are you always going out to save the world?" Questions Rayella, Lenard's fiancée.

Lenard kisses Rayella on her right cheek as he heads out into the dark night.

Rayella grabs her favorite coffee mug filled with wine and walks to her bedroom. She lays in bed and reaches for her alarm clock. After setting the alarm for 3am she relaxes in bed until she drifts away in dreamland.

The alarm rings loudly at 3am. Rayella, still tired and half asleep, extends her hand to the alarm and pushes it until it is silent. Less than thirty seconds later her phone rings.

"Like clockwork." Rayella mumbles as she answers her phone.

"You know me babe, did you fall asleep or were you awaiting my nightly call," asks Lenard.

"Boy bye, nobody is sitting around waiting on your call, you are not all that." Jokes Rayella.

The couple speaks on the phone for over an hour, until Lenard's dispatcher comes through. Lenton hangs up the phone with Rayella and answers the dispatcher.

"10-4," says Lenard to his dispatcher. He turns on his police sirens and drives downtown.

 He is the first officer on site.

There are phone cameras everywhere. Over twenty people are standing on the scene all with cameras in hand. Lenard walks towards the scene where he witnesses a man face down covered in his own blood. It is apparent that the person is dead. Lenard surveys the scene but sees no one other than bystanders with phones recording the body of the dead man lying on the concrete.

Unsure where to start, Lenard informs his dispatcher that he arrived, but sees no perpetrator in site.

He stays near the body until the paramedics arrive. Within minutes paramedics are on the scene and waste no time picking up the dead body of the man lying on the ground.

Lenard secures the scene with tape then heads back to the police station to complete his report.

Still not sure of what happened, other than someone dying, Lenard reports to his supervisor for clarity on what may have happened.

His supervisor, Earl, tells him to simply complete the report based off his view of what transpired and turn it in directly to him as he will handle the rest.

Lenard, a ten-year veteran with the police department asks no further questions and completes his report.

When his shift is over, he returns to the home he and his fiancée share. Rayella is awake watching her early morning shows when Lenard arrives.

Lenard greets his fiancée then, as he always does after a long shift, proceeds to his room for rest.

While he is walking towards the room Rayella screams. "No, how dare the news interrupt my show, I was just about to find out who the daddy was, this is bull shit."

Lenard, turns around to address her and her 'noise' when he sees himself on the television screen.

"Turn it up babe, turn it up hurry." Says Lenard.

On the news is the airing of a video taken by a bystander. It shows Lenard standing around waiting for the paramedics. The paramedics leave with the body, but the person who videoed the scene captured something peculiar. The video shows Earl in the driver seat of the ambulance.

"What in the world." Mumbles Lenard.

He then instructs Rayella to rewind the TV as he can't believe his eyes. Why would his supervisor be driving a paramedic's truck?

"This makes absolutely no sense." Says Lenard who picks up his cell phone to call his partner Shelly.

Shelly was not working last night as she was home sick. She answers on the first ring saying. "Oh my goodness, I was just about to call you. What happened last night?"

Lenard, who is still confused by what he witnessed on television says, "Someone died. He was dead when I got there. I don't know who did it or if there is even a lead on what occurred. I am just getting home, but did you see the news?"

"Yes," says Shelly. "I saw all of it. Check your phone I am about to send you the full video that has been circulating all morning long. Let me know when you get it."

"Yeah, ok, let me check it out I will call you back."
Says Lenard.

Lenard hangs up with his partner. Within a few seconds
a text message comes through on his phone.

It is a video. On the video is an altercation of a police
officer, whose identification is not clear. Along with a
black male who looks to be in his early twenties. The
police officer and male are seen talking then without
notice the police fires his gun towards the male and
leaves the scene.

Lenard replays the video over and over for an hour
minimum. He can't understand what is going on.

Lenard doesn't sleep though he is exhausted. Shelly
later calls him back to inform him she will be out again
tonight but because of what's going on he may need to
contact their supervisor for a partner, just to be safe.

Lenard is hesitant to contact his supervisor but does.
Earl tells Lenard that he needs to be at work at least
thirty minutes earlier than scheduled to speak with
public affairs and 'get his story straight'.

Lenard lays in bed most of the day without sleeping. He
later prepares for his night shift, kisses Rayella on her

right cheek and leaves home. When he arrives to the
police station it is a mad house. Everyone has saw the
video tapes circulating. Lenard asks a few people for
information on where public affairs officers are
stationed as he knows he has to speak with them. When
he goes in, Earl is also in the room.

Earl introduces Lenard to everyone in the room. "Now
go on, Lenard, tell everyone what you saw last night."

"Well," states Lenard. "I didn't see much. I received a
call from the dispatcher and I responded to the call.
Once arrived, I saw citizens recording and live
streaming the area. Everyone was surrounded by a body
lying on the ground. A man was dead lying in his own
blood. The paramedics arrived and left with the body
and well that was it. I stayed back and secured the scene
then came back to the office to complete and turn in my
report."

One of the officers who is a member of the public
affairs team asks, "Who were the paramedics?"

Lenard says without thought, "I didn't pay attention. It
was dark and they quickly picked up the body."

The same officer asks, "Where is your partner?"

"Shelly? She called in sick, she has been out for a few days now." Says Lenard.

The officers look at one another then they excuse Lenard from the room.

Lenard works his entire shift. He is extremely tired as he didn't sleep prior to work. At 3am he calls his fiancée as he always does and the two speak for a few hours.

When his shift is over, he returns home and falls into a deep sleep as he is beyond exhausted.

He sleeps the entire day, awaking only with enough time to prepare for work.

When he arrives at work Shelly is there. Happy to see his partner Lenard rushes over to her. Before he can speak, she looks at him with an angered look. "How could you? We have been partners for years, I looked up to you since I started and you reported me? When have you ever witnessed me driving a paramedic's truck? When? You know what, it doesn't even matter because we both know who the driver was and I will not stop until I get him and you out of this office."

Shelly walks off with a box of her belongings in hand.

She is escorted out of the police station by a detective.

Lenard is standing in a state of shock. He and Shelly spoke the day after the incident. He never reported her or even made mention of her on his report. He and her both knew it was their supervisor Earl in the driver seat. His hat was lowered and it was impossible to see him clearly as he never got out of the truck to help the two EMT's with the body but it was Earl. How could they even think it was Shelly? She does have a short haircut and Earl hates the fact that she is a woman on his team, but it still makes no sense. Earl often made jokes about her being a 'stud' and he is against same sex relationships but her personal life is not his business or anyone else's. Things just aren't adding up.

Lenard walks to Earl's office to get clarification. Earl is in his office with an FBI agent. "Lenard, you are off duty. You have been through plenty in the last few days and well, with everything going on with Shelly I know you need time to digest it all. The two of you have been partners for years. Go home, take the next few days off. We will see you next week.'

"Um," states Lenard. "I am sorry but did you get a chance to review my police report?"

"Yes, of course." States Earl as he stands to his feet.

"Thank you, everything has been handed over to the FBI, Enjoy your time off."

Lenard leaves the police station just as confused as ever.

He tries calling Shelly but her phone goes straight to voicemail.

Lenard arrives home and re-watches the videos streaming online over and over again.

He texted Shelly multiple times requesting a call back but was unsuccessful with a response.

He confides in his fiancée; she instructs him to report everything to the FBI.

Without hesitation, Lenard leaves home and drives to the nearest state trooper's unit as that office houses a few FBI agents in their building. There is no way he can talk to the police at his station with Earl physically there.

Lenard arrives at the state trooper's building only to discover that Earl is there.

Earl sees him instantly. "Lenard, you know I had a feeling you may come here and well I guess you almost ruined the surprise. Congratulations, you will receive a medal of honor for your work."

"I'm sorry but what?" Asks a demented Lenard.

"You heard me." says Earl. "You are amazing at your job; you deserve a medal of courage for all that you do. I mean It could not have been easy arriving to the scene alone and having to deal with all those citizens. We will formerly honor you next week. Can you at least act surprised?"

Earl and the other officers near him all laugh.

Lenard shrugs his shoulders then leaves.

After his few days off work, he is well rested and ready to return to work. Shelly still has not returned any of his calls. He is informed of his new partner, one who was a past marine and comes highly recommended but Lenard isn't impressed. He wants Shelly back as his partner.

Time passes and things are not the same. The young man killed that night has been buried. The police claimed it was self- defense due to the young man having a weapon which was never found, and Lenard still can't believe that Shelly somehow took the fall for his supervisor. What's worse is that Lenard can't figure out why Earl would even be driving the paramedic's truck in the first place. He isn't trained to do so. It isn't protocol. None of that night makes any sense.

Lenard puts in a request for extended time off. His wedding is now less than a month away and he is a wreck.

He is granted time off. He spent time at home doing nothing but staring at his award that was presented. Just as Earl said, he received an award; an award for nothing.

Lenard can't get the events of that night in question out of his head. There is a missing piece that no one seems to know and surprisingly no one seems to care. Why was Earl driving the paramedic truck, why did the police shoot the young man that night, what is going on?

Rayella, who is now worried about her fiancé sits down to have a conversation with him. "Lenard, I love you. I really do, but this is insane. Everyday all you do is stare at videos all day long looking for answers. If you feel something is wrong speak up. You owe it to not only Shelly but the guy who lost his life. It's such a sad story and yes, the media is just not helping by showing it daily but clearly this case is affecting you. What do you want to do? You can't just sit here daily and reflect. Life has to go on. Do you remember last year when Karen set you up and attempted to get you fired by starting a bogus sexual harassment claim simply because she wanted your shift? You fought back right? Karen tried to pull every trick in the book to get rid of you but you stood your ground. You never missed a beat. Instead, you worked harder to prove yourself and, in the end, everything worked in your favor and Karen's vindictive ways caught up with her. This situation though different in occurrence is similar. You have to fight. Lenard you are such an intelligent man; you always do what's right. You need to release in an effort to get past this. We both know that Shelly was not involved. We have known her and her family for years and you know she was at home sick. You know she is being framed and targeted for reasons unknown. I don't have all the answers, I wish I did. But this has to stop. Call 911. Call the FBI. Call someone, anyone please. Tell them what you know. It was Earl that night driving, only he knows the reason why, maybe it was to protect the officer involved, or maybe he is doing some illegal dealings at the police station but either way something is going on and it's not right. A dead man's blood is on your hands. You have to step up."

Rayella then leans close to Lenard and says, "I love you and I know you will do the right thing; you always do."

She leaves Lenard alone to think. He has a million thoughts flowing through his head.

Time passes by. It is nearly a month since the tragic night that took the life of a black man now identified as a young man with hopes and dreams of becoming a medical doctor. A young man with no prior issues, no concerns. A man who in fact was not armed on that fatal night.

Lenard has been driving himself crazy. He can't take it anymore. It is now only two days before his wedding and just knowing that Earl and the police who killed the young man are both at work carrying on as though nothing happened makes Lenard's skin crawl.

Lenard prays, meditates, and decides that he needs to come clean. His police report was clearly altered once he submitted it to Earl. Shelly was terminated and is now facing possible prosecution for the crime of another and a man is dead for no reason known to anyone.

Lenard leaves home and drives to the scene of the place the crime occurred. He sits in his car then attempts to contact Shelly; no answer.

Lenard slowly drives to the police station. Regardless of who is there he knows he has to come clean. He has to be an officer of dignity and respect.

As he enters the police station, he bypasses Earls' office and notices it is empty. It is bare, all of Earl's pictures have been taken off the wall. The office has nothing inside but a chair, desk, and computer.

Relieved that justice has started to unfold, Lenard takes out his phone to contact his fiancée as he can't wait to tell her, when he is stopped by a co-worker. "We have a new police chief."

"Really?" Says a hopeful Lenard as he saves his phone. "But that is so odd, why with everything going on would someone want to be hired in this mess. It doesn't even make sense. This office never hires in this type of manner. The police chief position has been open for quite some time but the office seemed to not want to rush and hire anyone, especially with the media coverage surrounding such a tragic death."

Lenard walks to the police chief's office and there he was the new police chief; Earl.

Lenard literally can't move. How is Earl now the boss. It was one thing when Earl was a supervisor and the leading officer but now, he is the entire police station's boss.

Earl witnesses Lenard staring at him. "Lenard, how is life treating you? I hope you are enjoying your time off. I wanted to call you. The other officers and I are all going to the old camp reserve down the hill in a few months. It's been a lot to take in over the last month and well, we all need a break. Do you remember Karen? Well, her husband owns property down the hill and she said she would arrange everything. You know I think she feels bad for how things went down with the whole harassment allegation case. She specifically asked if you would be coming with us to the cabin. She said she wants to 'catch up' with you. That may be a good chance to talk and smooth things over. A nice cabin, light some candles, and well you can decide what you want to do with her." Earl nudges Lenard while laughing then says, "Listen, I am not supposed to tell you this yet, but congratulations. You are now the supervising officer. The decision was made late last night. There isn't a doubt in my mind, you are the best man for the job. I know you can handle everything that comes your way; my old position is now yours."

Lenard is shellshocked. He is standing in place saying nothing.

Earl is staring at Lenard. "Did you hear me? Are you okay? You have been promoted. You can move into your new office as soon as you return from your honeymoon.

Lenard is frozen in thought.

"Say, what are you doing here anyway? You aren't scheduled to return to work until after your honeymoon." Says Earl with an eyebrow raised.

"Oh yeah," Lenard answers. "Um, I just stopped by um, I just stopped by to invite you to my upcoming wedding; don't be late. It starts at 4pm, bring a gift."

The day of his wedding, Lenard journals his thoughts….

We all have a voice. It's not my business, it's never my place. Damn who am I to dictate what happens with the human race. I am merely one person, no one will understand. They will look and stare proclaiming I am a snitch. I will just keep my mouth shut forgetting that I have rights; damn why did I have to be there that night. I don't want to say anything. I just want life to be normal. Maybe someone else will speak. Dear Lord, please let the truth come out in an unforeseen video leak.

We Woke Up

A Night to Regret

"Like seriously, $400.00 for a dress that is just absurd."
Yells Dina as she and her best friends Brittany and
Kylie are shopping for dresses to wear at their
twentieth-year high school reunion.

"No what is absorb is the fact that our twentieth-year
class reunion is in less than four hours and Kylie
actually waited until the last minute, as usual, to pick up
something to wear." Smirks Brittany.

Kylie playfully rolls her eyes at her friends.

Kylie is now shouting across the aisles. "Hey you guys
don't forget next weekend is my dad's retirement party.
After forty years of service, he is finally retiring from
the jewelry store and he deserves a celebration. I mean
after all he manages the most expensive jewelry store in
the bayou."

Dina is seemingly excited. "We will definitely be there.
I already have his retirement gift in the trunk of my
car."

Brittany's cell phone rings. "Hello? What, oh no that is
ridiculous I put in my request weeks ago you will just

have to find someone else to work tonight because I can't, not tonight. What? But why?"

Brittany hangs up the phone and is now upset. "Can you believe it I have to go to work tonight."

Kylie and Dina yell. "What?"

Brittany shrugs. "So apparently both of the night nurses quit and one of them was the on-call person but since she is gone it rolls over to next week and of course the next on call person is me."

Dina is being very sarcastic as she says, "Can't they find someone else? We have had this night planned for almost a year and besides I hardly ever get to get out without Tony."

Brittany is looking disappointed. "You know I was looking forward to tonight but I can't afford to not go in and lose my job. I am sorry guys, I hate to be the 'party pooper' but I have to leave and try to get a few hours of rest before my twelve-hour shift, sorry." She gives a sad smirk then walks out of the store.

Dina wastes no time. "Well Kylie looks like it's just me and you. I need to be home early to tuck Dole in bed before I leave."

Kylie who is still shopping looks to her friend, "Go on ahead, I just have a few more items to pick up. I can meet you tonight at seven outside of the reunion, near the front entrance, cool?"

Dina agrees, she leaves the store and heads home.

Dina who is a mother to a toddler drives homes as fast as she can to have quality time with her son Dole before leaving for the night.

After arriving home, she feeds and tends to her son. She then tucks him in for the night. "Dole, mommy loves you so much. Be good for daddy okay." As Dina hugs her son in walks her husband Tony.

"Hey babe." Says Tony with a smile. "It's almost 7pm you are going to be late."

Dina while staring at her son says to her husband, "I'm leaving, take care of my baby boy and please make sure he eats breakfast in the morning and I don't mean cookies either, feed him a healthy breakfast."

Tony chuckles. "He will be fine. Call me later when you and your friends make it to the hotel so that I know that you are okay."

Dina hugs her husband then proceeds to leave for the

evening. Dina arrives to the reunion prior to Kylie. She refreshes her lipstick then waits for her friend near the front entrance of the school gym; where the reunion is held. While waiting, an old high school classmate passes by and stops to chat.

Dina looks and recognizes her classmate. "Oh, my goodness, hi, how are you?"

Dina and her classmate 'catch up'. They talk about their families as well as current events. Dina's classmate inquires of work.

Dina laughs. "Well, I wish I could stay home daily, but I actually work at the federal bank not far from here."

Her friend is impressed and inquires of her position at the bank.

Dina proudly says, "I am a bank teller."

Her friend looks in disgust then makes an excuse to end the conversation.

Just as her high school friend leaves Dina's phone rings; it's Kylie.

"Kylie?" asks Dina. "Where are you it's after 7pm and …. what…what are you talking about? What emergency? What happened? Kylie? Hello?"

Kylie hung up the phone leaving Dina upset, "Oh just great she has a family emergency, just great! There is no way I am walking in the reunion alone, especially not after running into that fool. Oh well I guess I will go and enjoy my hotel suite, after all it's already paid for."

Dina who has convinced herself not to walk in the reunion alone decides to leave and check into the hotel. Once settled in her hotel room, she is still dressed, playing online looking for something to do.

"What to do, what to do," mumbles Dina. "I have make-up on, I look good, and I may not have the chance to get away anytime soon so I need to make the most of it, but what can I do……." She is strolling on her cell phone. "Hmmm what do we have here? Meet local singles, only one call away, hmm, oh well what the hell. What's the worst that can happen." Dina dials the number and begins to talk. "Let's see it says hit 1 for the next voice or 2 to speak live to someone, let's live a little Dina." She hits the key to talk with someone. "Hello, Hi I am Dina how are you, come over? What? But I didn't even get your name? Oh, why thank you most people I talk to say I have a sexy voice, really, oh stop, yes, I am alone, why? Come over, you are a persistent one aren't you, no I don't think so, what? Oh, stop it, who are you Mr. Prince Charming? Yeah right; ok but just for a few minutes, I need to see who I am speaking with. I am at the hotel near the high school on third street in, what yes that's the one, wow you are already in the area, ok well I am in room 204, see you soon."

Dina hangs up, panics for a second then takes a deep breath. Within a few minutes there is a knock on the door. Dina opens it and looks at the man from head to toe and then begins to blush. He is very muscular, with a long torso. You can see his abs under his very tight t-shirt. The guy has a very low fade and an earring in both ears. He has a tattoo with a rose that flows all the way down his right arm to his wrist. He smiles and his dimples are as deep as the ocean. He is a sight for sore eyes and Dina is smitten.

Dina welcomes the guy inside her room but as she closes the hotel room door Dina notices he has a small black leather overnight bag that he is carrying. Dina and the guy go inside, yet he has not properly introduced himself. She is on the edge of the bed. Meanwhile he is sitting in a chair with his bag near him, the two make small talk.

Dina wants to break the ice. "So, um what are you doing in the area, wait I am so sorry but I didn't catch your name."

The guy is silent for a second. "Oh, really my name is….is that a banker's mug? I love that bank."

Dina responds. "Um yes, yes, it is I actually work at the bank."

The guy is intrigued. "Really how interesting."

Dina responds. "Actually, it's not I am just a bank teller."

The guy looks at her and in his deep yet soothing voice says, "Don't ever down play what you do, as long as you like it and it pays the bills that is all that matters. Say, what can a brother do to get one of those mugs."

Dina stands up and gets a business card out of her wallet. "This is my card, just call the bank during the week and we can get you one." Dina hands him the card then sits back on the edge of the bed.

The guy places the card in his pocket. "So, what do you want to do tonight……."

Dina looks at him then looks down as though she is

embarrassed. He notices and sits beside her. He places his right hand over hers. Dina can't believe how good he smells. She gently leans closer to him as his smell is so refreshing. He then removes his hand from hers and pulls her in closer. The two say no words, instead they begin to kiss. One thing leads to another and Dina and the guy who she has yet to get to know are now both in her bed.

The next morning Dina's phone is ringing. She wakes up and notices her guest is sleeping shirtless beside her, she ignores her phone but it rings continuously.

Dina, unable to ignore the ring, answers the phone. "Hello? Tony hi, how are you this morning? What here? Where? In the hotel?" At this point Dina is standing up shocked while her male guest is still sleeping. Umm room number umm what umm where is Dole, oh my um what no of course I know my room number it's room 204, huh? I mean yeah see you in a minute."

Dina wakes up her guest and begins to kick him out. She grabs his shirt and is pushing him towards the door. He grabs his shirt from her and he is yelling that he needs his bag but she keeps pushing him out. Dina looks around to make sure the room is clean but then she sees the black bag brought in by her male guest. Dina forces the bag in her large green suitcase to hide it from her husband. There is a knock at the door. Dina opens the door. It is her husband and son with a box of donuts.

Her son yells, "Surprise mommy."

They walk in the hotel room.

Tony is looking around the room. "What happened?"

Dina is now nervous. "Huh? Who-who-what are you talking about?"

Tony grins. "Last night you were supposed to call me when you got in. I decided to take Dole out for donuts and we ran into Brittany. She told me she had to work and you were here so we decided to come and bring donuts. Where is Kylie? We brought enough donuts for both of you?!"

Dina has to think fast. "Oh, uh she had to leave early."

"Awe well it is a good thing we came to keep you company." Tony says as he kisses his wife on the forehead.

Dina's phone rings shortly after.

"Hello, hey Kylie, I met to call you is everything okay? What?" Dina turns to Tony and says, "Tony, turn on the tv to the news."

Tony, with the remote in hand doesn't know what he is looking for.

Dina has now ended her call with her friend. "I am not sure what channel but that was Kylie. Her dad, well he works at the jewelry store and it was robbed and he was shot last night. He just passed away at the hospital."

Tony walks up to his wife and hugs her. Dole is playing with a toy on the floor nearby the entire time.

Dina and her family leave the hotel. She later calls Brittany and the two friends decide to visit Kylie to show their respect.

Brittany and Dina ride together. Once they arrive, they get out of the car to visit with Kylie who is sitting outside her dad's home. The three ladies greet with a hug and sit down.

Brittany breaks the ice. "Oh Kylie, I am so sorry for your loss. I know how close you and your dad were. Oh, if there is anything you need at all I am here for you, we both are."

Dina gently grabs Kylie's hand as Kylie is in tears.

Kylie, in between tears says, "I just can't believe it, forty years at that jewelry store and no incidents and a week before he is set to retire, he is robbed and shot dead. It is just too much, I- I." Kylie is crying uncontrollably. Her friends console her.

Kylie wipes her eyes with a napkin. "I am sorry, I am okay. Dina, please tell me all about the reunion."

Dina is looking surprised. "Oh no, no I can't this just is not the time, we are here for you and…."

She is cut off by Kylie. "No, please, I want to hear about it, I need to get my mind on something other than my dad right now, please tell us all about it."

Dina shrugs. "Well, if you insist, the truth is I didn't go to the reunion."

Kylie and Brittany both looked confused.

Dina grins then says, "Kylie after you called, I just couldn't go in there alone, I was just too embarrassed to walk in solo, so I went back to the hotel and …. I ……met up with someone."

Brittany is now really confused. "Someone as in your

husband? You don't know nobody but us girl."

Dina laughs before mumbling. "Someone as in a stranger."

Brittany and Kylie are now sitting with their mouth wide open in disbelief.

Dina isn't shocked by the reaction of her friends as Dina is a strait-laced loving wife and mother. "I was bored and I kind of wanted to just let loose and enjoy my night so I called a chat line, chatted with a male, and then kind of invited him over for the night. I know it was wrong but I just couldn't resist and well, never mind."

Brittany is now standing on her feet. "You have truly lost your mind. Is this some type of joke? Like really? You? Queen of the, 'I got a husband and I can't stay out past 8pm'?! This must be a joke. Is today April 1st because this must be an April fool's joke."

Dina is no longer smiling. "It's not a joke. I messed up. It was only supposed to be a few minutes with him to talk and pass the time but before I knew it, we were in bed together and he was kissing me and well one thing led to another and well, I kind of had a one-night stand."

There is silence.

Dina can't take the quietness. "Well, say something. Oh, what have I done? I don't even know his name and I slept with him."

Brittany is shaking her head.

 "Well," says Kylie sarcastically. "That certainly got my mind off of my dad."

Seconds later Dina's phone goes off, it's an alert.

Dina, looking at her phone, "Oh my goodness, I can't believe it, I just got an interview with Edwards and Associates Enterprises."

Kylie with her arms crossed says, "No offense Dina but what are you trying to go do over there, don't they do corporate budgets and project management?"

Dina slightly nudges her friend. "Um yes, they do, but the funny thing is that they reached out to me. I was online earlier and I received an email about a position and all I had to do was send my resume. I sent it in and now they just alerted me that I have an interview on tomorrow with the CEO of the company."

"What's the position," asks Brittany as she is intrigued.

Dina looks at her friend. "Who knows and who cares it's an interview with the CEO, wow I can't believe it."

Brittany who seemingly knows everything about Dina says, "I didn't know you were trying to leave the bank."

"Well, I wasn't," admits Dina. "But then I don't know. I guess if something better came along, I would take it, I mean I can't be a bank teller forever."

The three friends visit for a few hours. Just speaking of memories of Kylie's dad and good times they have shared. They later leave and return to their own homes.

A few days passes and the time has come for Dina's interview. She is extremely nervous yet excited for such an opportunity to interview for a prestigious company but she doesn't want to get her hopes up too high.

Dina arrives at the interview site and is escorted to a conference room. She is instructed to sit at the table and await the CEO, Karen.

Karen enters. She is a slim lady with very long straight blonde hair. Her nails are beautifully manicured and she is wearing the nicest high heels Dina has ever seen.

Karen introduces herself as she is looking over Dina's resume, then leads the interview.

After a short interview Karen extends her hand to Dina and offers her the job on the spot. Dina willingly accepts the position.

Once Dina leaves, she calls her husband to tell him the good news, then her friends. Though Kylie is extremely happy she is unable to talk long as she is assisting with her dad's estate since he is gone. Brittany is home doing nothing and insists that she and Dina go out to dinner to celebrate.

Dina and Brittany decide to go out to dinner the same night as Tony had already promised to take he and Dina's son to an event for some 'father son time.'

While walking to their table, once they arrived at the restaurant Dina sees Karen and her husband.

Karen gave Dina the cold shoulder and made it clear she does not care to speak with her employees outside of the office.

Dina is a little taken back by Karen but she doesn't give it a second thought.

A few moments later Dina's phone rings, it's an unknown number.

Knowing something is wrong based on Dina's facial

expression, Brittany inquires of the call.

Dina says, "I started getting these weird calls lately. I picked up yesterday and it was a call from the county jail."

Brittany with a startled look, asks who the caller was.

"I don't know", says Dina. "I always hang up before the person speaks to say their name. Yesterday Tony and I were watching Dole play soccer and there were five calls from that same number."

Brittany tells her friend, "Girl it is probably the wrong number. Next time they call answer it and let them know they are calling the wrong person so that they can stop calling your phone."

Dina's phone rings again.

Brittany insists Dina put it on speaker.

It is a call from the county jail.

Both friends look at each other.

Dina accepts the call.

The caller speaks Dina's name. "Dina why haven't you been accepting my calls?"

Dina unsure who the caller is says, "You must have the wrong number sir."

"Sir? Oh, so we are formal now? It wasn't sir when I was laying in your bed licking all over your body at the hotel now was it?" Proclaims the male caller.

Dina's mouth opens wide before asking the caller how he obtained her number.

"Don't worry about all that where is my bag?" Asks the male caller.

Dina asks, "What? A bag? You blowing up my damn phone for a fucking bag?"

"Look, I need my bag. Now I will give you an address where to mail it and I will pick it up from the address in a few days, all you need to do is go…."

Dina hangs up while he is talking.

Dina looks at Brittany and sarcastically says, "Girl that fool is crazy, I am not mailing no bag, he is stupid to be blowing up my phone like that."

Dina's phone rings again.

Dina looks and it is the same number. "Really, he is

calling again, I am going to politely block him. Now we can enjoy our evening, cheers to my new career."

The two friends toast their glasses and proceed to drink wine.

They enjoy the remainder of their evening then return to their homes as it is a weekday and Dina has a full agenda prior to starting her new job.

A few weeks go by and all is well.

The day finally comes for Dina to start her new job. She arrives at the office and enters a meeting with Karen and team members; Dina walks in late.

Karen refrains from talking when Dina opens the door. Karen looks at Dina and angrily says, *"YOU ARE LATE."*

Dina tries to explain. "I am so sorry, someone tried to break in my house this morning and it was just awful, I am so sorry…."

Karen interrupts her and instructs her to have a seat.

Dina sits down.

Karen restarts speaking but Dina's phone rings loudly.

Dina hits ignore.

Karen breathes heavily then proceeds to speak.

Dina's phone is ringing yet again, she presses ignore.

Karen continues addressing the team. "We are exceeding our forecasted budget and I believe that we…."

Dina's phone rings again, she turns it completely off.

Karen is now aggravated and asks Dina if she needs to be reminded of company policy while in meetings.

Dina is embarrassed. "No, no you don't I am sorry someone keeps calling me from different numbers."

Dina is now sitting at attention. Because her phone is now turned off, she is able to concentrate.

The remainder of her work day is surprisingly well.

She later returns home for an evening with her family.

Dina and her family are having dinner when the doorbell rings. Since her husband is helping their son by cutting the meat on his plate Dina opens the door. When she opens it, the guy from the hotel is standing in her doorway.

Dina is frantically freaking out.

"Where is my bag?" He asks.

"Shh," whispers Dina. "Keep your voice down! Get off of my property *NOW*."

He grabs her arm and says, "I will leave soon as I get my bag."

Dina pushes his hand off of her arm. "My husband is home; you will have to wait. I will get it out of the attic in the morning."

Second later Tony yells, "Honey who is at the door?"

Dina, trying to think fast says, "Huh oh it's the neighbor. I ordered some candles from her but the order isn't in yet."

Tony, though not remembering his wife ordering candles, continues assisting his son.

"I need my bag." Utters the guy.

Dina then asks, "Wait weren't you in jail? How did you even get out?"

"Lack of evidence." He then grins.

"What?" Dina asks confused. "Wait, how did you get my address? You know what, never mind, I don't even care just never come here again." She then abruptly slams the door in his face, only to have him ring the doorbell again.

She quickly opens the door slightly.

The man looks at Dina and says, "You have 24 hours to get my bag or else!"

Dina closes the door, takes a deep breath, then returns to dinner.

Tony, who has no idea what is going on, asks what took so long.

Dina is now scrambling in her chair. "Oh, nothing just trying to help the neighbor figure out ways to sell more candles."

Dina and her family finish their dinner and enjoy a night of television movies.

The next morning Dina is pacing the floor waiting for Tony to leave for work so she can get the black bag. However, Tony is reading the paper lounging on the sofa without a care in the world.

Dina now getting nervous tries to rush him out of the house.

Tony looks at her and says, "Remember I told you today is the annual field trip, my aide is bringing the students. I am going to meet them there so I have a few hours to relax."

Dina totally forgot about the pre-scheduled field trip. She tries to figure a way to get her husband out of the house. "Umm O I see, umm well can you bring Dole to preschool for me that way I can get to work early? I have so much to do today."

Tony who has nothing planned until it's time to go to work agrees.

Dina is pacing back and forth, waiting for them to leave. Dole is dressed for school waiting when the doorbell rings.

Dina, scared it's the guy yells, "I got it."

Tony screams back. "No, I am already up I got it. Relax why are you so jumpy this morning!?"

The guy has returned and he is at the door when Tony opens it.

Tony, who never met the guy before greets him. "Hello, how can I help you?"

The guy wastes no time talking, "Yeah, hi I met your wife a few weeks ago and she has something that belongs to me and I need it now."

Tony is now intrigued. "Excuse me, you met my wife? Who are you and when did you meet Dina?"

Dina then runs to the door with a box in her hand.

"Oh Tony," says an out of breath Dina. "This is my co-worker um well my old coworker well not old but he took my place at the bank and I told him to come by and I would give him items that I accidently left with. Here, here you go I didn't get a chance to get all the items from the attic but I promise you I will as soon as I can. I have just been so busy."

Dina hands the guy a box then rushes and closes the door.

Tony now with his arms crossed says, "Dina what in the world was that all about?"

Dina, who is now scared straight says, "Nothing dear, you and Dole will be late I will talk to you later."

Tony senses something is wrong. "No Dina, you will talk to me now. Ever since the reunion you have been jumpy. What is wrong with you?"

Dina lies telling her husband she is fine.

Tony, is not buying it and insists his wife communicate with him.

"Tony I, I got to go, I will be late for work." Dina says while trying to hold it together. She is in such a hurry that she forgets to kiss her son goodbye.

Tony sits down and looks confused.

Dina arrives on time at the office for the morning meeting.

Karen is standing at the head of the conference table and addresses the team. "Well team we have done it again, it looks like we are forecasted to meet our annual budget." Everyone claps. "I wanted to do something special, you all have worked so hard this year and well I thought I should do something nice for you in return. As you know because we have met goals you will each receive a bonus and as always, I will ensure that I hand deliver them to you so that you don't have to patiently wait by the mailbox." Everyone in the room laughs. "In addition to your bonus that is coming, I reached out to the most exclusive hotel resort in the area, and I told them of your hard work and well they decided to give me a hotel stay free of charge; all perks included. I had my assistant put all of your names in a raffle and one lucky person will have the remainder of the day off with pay, along with a hotel stay at the resort with your family tonight. The person selected for the hotel stay is Dina."

Dina is shocked yet extremely excited.

Karen with a smile says, "Congratulations Dina, you have the rest of the day off to go and pack for your overnight stay at the hotel; enjoy."

"I am so excited," Dina says happily. "I am getting off early enough to make it to the store, there is this potted plant I want to purchase for my friend."

Karen mumbles, "A potted plant?"

Dina says, "Yes, my friend loss her dad less than a month ago. I want to get her a plant to help brighten her day."

Karen is clicking her ink pen, "Interesting…."

Dina walks out of the meeting to call her husband but

he doesn't answer, she leaves a voice mail. Dina rushes to purchase a plant then returns home to pack for the night's stay. Her husband was apprehensive about leaving the house for an overnight stay during the week, but ultimately Dina convinced him that it was too good of a deal to pass by.

Dina and her family arrive to the hotel; it's simply beautiful. There is a full waterfall in the front lobby. A spa, fitness center, bar, swimming area, 24-hour restaurant, and a mini shopping mall; all inside the hotel resort.

Once checked in the room Dina apologizes to her husband for her 'jumpy' attitude the last few weeks and assures him she loves him and things will be better.

She, her husband, and son watch movies together. They fall asleep fairly early but wake up with enough time the next morning to enjoy some of the hotel amenities.

When it is time to return to work Dina is refreshed and happy but then right when she opens the door for the meeting at work her phone rings.

Dina apologizes. "I am sorry, it's an unknown number during the school day, it could be my son's school. I have to take this call."

Dina steps out of the meeting and answers the call.

A male's voice is on the other line. Dina immediately knows it is the same guy that has been harassing her.

Dina is now pleading with him. "Please, please leave me alone. Please I just want to be alone, I am so sorry about your bag. Please I just want my life back."

After a quick silence, the guy says, "Your wish is my command…. Good-bye Dina."

He then surprisingly hangs up. Dina goes in the meeting shaking and hysterical.

Dina still shaken up says, "I, I am sorry. I just, I don't know what to do anymore he just won't stop." Dina puts her head in her hand and starts to cry.

Everyone is staring at Dina who is literally crying uncontrollably. Meanwhile Karen is getting annoyed.

Karen gives Dina a second to gather herself but Dina can't seem to stop crying. Karen then instructs the team to leave the room.

Dina and Karen are now alone in the conference room.

Karen, without an ounce of feelings says, "Dina, when

you started at this corporation, I told you that you only had one chance. You are the newest associate here yet you have the most drama. I am running a business! Now I understand that your life is not peaches and cream but the office is no place to bring your dirty laundry. Dina…"

Dina looks up at Karen.

Karen crosses her arms and firmly says, "You are fired. You have five minutes to get your ungrateful ass out of my office."

Dina is shocked.

Karen proceeds to exit the conference room.

Dina, still crying says, "What?! Fired?! Wait what? What for? I huh? I am fired?"

Before opening the conference door to exit Karen looks at Dina and says, "Turn in your key at the front desk."

Dina stands and begins to speak as she knows Karen is walking out and this may be her final chance to fight for her job. "I need my job Karen. I ended a ten-year job at the bank for this job. I come in early, most days, I stay late at your request as needed. I have never violated any policies. I complete all of my projects and you are firing me….”

Dina is interrupted by Karen.

“Pull yourself together Dina. Like I said this is a business. You are a grown woman coming to work day after day crying over harassing phone calls and whining to your co-workers about a black bag? Are you serious? Get your things and *GET OUT.*”

Karen then turns and walks away. Dina sits at the table and is upset. After a few minutes of confusion Dina begins talking to herself out loud. “Wait I never told her or anyone else about the bag. I never even told my closet friends; no one. How did she know? What is going on?”

Dina tries to go to Karen’s office but she is stopped by a co-worker and asked if she needs help.

Dina’s coworker informs her that Karen just left as she said she was going home early.

Dina then runs and tries to stop Karen. She sees Karen in the parking lot in her car. Karen makes eye contact then pulls out of the driveway.

Dina gets on her phone and calls the police.

"Hello is this the police, I need to make a report can I do it over the phone? Well yes, I can still come in to formally complete it but it's urgent. I think my boss is after me. I don't know all of that can you send an officer here please? I am outside the office, 4635 Fairyview Lane, yes that is the correct building I will be waiting outside for an officer."

Dina hangs up with the police dispatcher and feels as though she needs to tell someone; she calls Brittany.

Dina spills her guts out to her friend.

A Police officer arrives and Dina tries to explain how she thinks her boss is harassing her but she has little to no proof other than being fired. Dina tries to explain that Karen knew of the 'black bag' and she must have tried to set her up for not returning it.

The police officer is getting agitated and reminds Dina that it is a crime to file a fake police report.

Dina begs the police to do a follow up check at Karen's address.

The police officer does not know what to do but because Karen is well known in the city, he agrees to conduct a 'courtesy' visit just to check things out.

The police officer arrives at Karen's house. Dina followed the police trailing him a few cars back without him knowing.

The police proceed to knock on the door. Karen answers wearing a robe.

Karen greets the police. The police asks Karen if she has or knows of any bags that may be missing from Dina.

Karen wastes no time responding. "Umm no, I don't have anything of hers, where would I have gotten this bag from?"

Dina, runs towards the door and says, "You left work early because you know. Tell the officer please."

Keren looking puzzled says, "I know what? And since when is it a crime to leave work early to spend time with my husband?"

Karen's husband comes out without a shirt on questioning if everything is okay.

The officer extends his hand to Karen. "Good day ma'am, sorry to have bothered you."

Dina is now screaming. "Arrest her, arrest her, she set

me up I can feel it."

The officer literally has to remove Dina from the premises. Karen grins as she closes the door to her home.

Dina returns home with a warning about her behavior from the police. Once home, she and her husband are talking about their day. Dina doesn't mention the fact that she was fired. After a few hours at home there is a knock at the door; it's the police.

Tony answers the door.

The police officer checks out the surroundings once he is given permission to step inside.

He eyeballs Dina.

The police officer informs her that there was an anonymous call to the station about expensive jewelry that was reported stolen being in Dina's possession.

Dina is now confused. "My possession, um I am not following what do you mean?"

The police still looking around the home while standing near the door points his hand and asks, "Ma'am is that your potted plant?"

Dina quickly answers. "Yes, I bought it for a friend but I have been too busy to bring it to her."

The police, once permitted by Dina, puts gloves on and checks the potted plant.

Shortly after searching the plant an expensive looking diamond necklace is retrieved. He verifies the engraving then puts the necklace in a Ziploc bag.

The police sternly look at Dina and informs her that she is under arrest for robbery and murder!

Dina is taken by what the officer just stated.

The police officer proceeds to handcuff Dina; her husband is shocked and befuddled. The police leave with Dina immediately after reading her rights.

Tony follows the officer and Dina out of the home assuring Dina he will be following her to the police station.

Tony brings their son to a neighbor, who has babysat Dole before. He then proceeds to the police station. Dina is in a questioning room. Dina is sitting in the room crying when an attorney and her husband enters the room.

Tony rushes to his wife's side and embraces her.

Dina is emotional as no one has given her additional information on what is going on!

The attorney who is an old college friend of Tony was contacted to bring forth clarity. "Dina, I will be representing you but I need all of the details. I will need to ensure that I am prepared to help you."

Dina is fighting tears. "I understand. But I am just so confused, it's like since I started working my new job everything started going wrong. I mean I don't even know where to start I am so confused."

Her attorney removes a small notepad from his briefcase. "Let's start with the basic information. Where were you on the night of the jewelry store robbery. During that robbery a man was murdered. The time was approximately 7:10pm. Give me a second, I can bring up the jewelry store address, it is the one near the high school here in town. The only high school that isn't a private institution, hold on a sec, I have the address near."

Dina informs him that she is aware of the robbery and murder as she knew the man that was murdered. She informs her attorney that she was at a hotel at the approximate time he inquired.

Tony injects himself in the conversation, reminding his wife she was at the reunion during that time.

Dina, now embarrassed and not sure how to address her actual whereabouts, is unable to speak.

Her attorney, who is trying to piece together this puzzle of events needs the details. He asks Dina specifically where she was at that exact time.

Dina musters up the strength to speak. "I was at the hotel. I left the reunion early."

Tony slowly removes his arms from around his wife as the attorney responds. "So, you were at the hotel? Do you have the receipt? I will need to confirm the check-in time."

Dina defensively questions why the attorney acts as though he doesn't believe her.

Her attorney reminds her that he is on her side, however he needs every shred of evidence to convince the jury that she is not responsible of such a crime.

Dina pulls herself together but informs her attorney she doesn't have her phone to get the receipt.

Tony pulls out his phone.

Tony, while searching on his phone reminds his wife, he can pull up receipts through their hotel loyalty program.

Dina looks worried.

Tony clicks a few buttons. "There it is, you checked in at 7:14pm. Dina did you even go to the reunion?"

 Dina lies and insists she went to the reunion but left early.

Her attorney questions her about having any visitors or witnesses from her hotel stay. Dina defensively denies.

The attorney's phone rings. He then asks Dina if she has a spare key to their house anywhere.

Tony informs him that their neighbor who is a longtime family friend has a spare, as she babysits Dole.

The attorney proceeds to finish his phone conversation. "Ok, sure thank you and please let me know soon as it's complete."

He hangs up the phone and to Tony and Dina states, "The judge just issued a search warrant of your home.

Dina, we can't afford any surprises."

Dina ensures him that she has nothing to hide.

Her attorney grins. "Ok well all should be well. I will work on asking the judge to set your bail until you go to court. I will also recommend a speedy trial. No since in dragging this case out if you are innocent."

Dina was able to post bail within 24 hours. Once back home she had ample time to come clean to her husband about the events that occurred the night of her reunion but Dina could not build up the nerve.

Her attorney's request for a speedy trial was granted. Though it felt like years to Dina as she was out of work and putting on a façade every day for her family, the trial actually started within a few short months.

On the first day of the trial surprisingly the state's attorney calls the police officer dispatched to Dina when she called from her office to the stand.

The officer is asked to tell the court about a report that was made by Dina in recent weeks.

The officer under oath discusses the 'black bag' that Dina accused her boss of taking and her irate behavior in her boss' yard. The officer also informs the court that no 'black bag' was discovered during the search of the home of any sort.

Dina's attorney cross examines the officer. He asks about fingerprints from the jewelry recovered from Dina's home.

The officer without hesitation says, "No, the jewelry was deep inside the potted plant, no fingerprints could be found."

Dina's attorney has no further questions.

The state's attorney informs the court they have a witness whom turned in a statement to the police. A witness actually spotted a person running with a black bag near the hotel on the night of question. That proves that the 'black bag' does exist and the fact that Dina is aware of the bag further proves that she may be heavily involved in the crime that took place.

The judge calls a brief recess.

During the recess Dina is reminded by her attorney that she is next up on the stand.

After the short recess the judge calls the courtroom to order.

Dina's attorney calls her to the stand as he is certain that because there were no credible witnesses who could actually identify her as the person with the bag, Dina will be able to save herself and the trial will be over in record time.

Dina approaches the stand.

When her attorney questions her about committing robbery and murder she confidently denies it. She also denies having enemies as she lives a very private life.

Her attorney asks her to tell the court what she did on the night in question.

Dina addresses the court. "Well, I briefly went to my high school reunion then left early and went to my hotel room for the night. My husband and son came to meet me the next morning."

Dina's attorney has no further questions.

The state's attorney approaches.

The state's attorney wastes no time asking Dina what weapon she used to commit murder.

The judge states that the state's attorney is out of line.

The state's attorney apologizes, "Sorry let's start off slowly. You told the officer when you made the report of harassment on your boss that there was a black bag. The witness said she saw someone running near your exact hotel by the high school, not far from the jewelry store, with a black bag. The crime possibly occurred after you left the reunion. You were reportedly alone in your hotel room throughout the night with no one to witness your whereabouts. According to the hotel clerk you completed a quick check-in and never went to the front desk. If that is correct it is possible that you did a quick check-in with your smartphone which could be done from any location. How do you explain that?"

Dina is at a loss at how the state attorney is approaching the case but firmly denies any involvement.

The state's attorney then asks about the 'black bag' she was referring to when she called 911 and spoke with the officer.

Dina lowers her head.

The state's attorney reminds Dina she is under oath.

Dina is now crying.

The judge insists that Dina answer all questions asked.

Dina pauses as she is sobbing. She then looks at her husband who is sitting in the crowd. "I, I am so sorry honey I love you so much and I…." She is unable to continue as she is emotional.

Her husband is looking confused.

The state's attorney is getting impatient.

Dina is still crying when the judge instructs her to answer the question asked.

Dina gains composure. "I met someone."

Everyone including Dina's attorney is stunned.

Dina continues, "I met someone and he came over and he spent the night and he forgot his black bag. I don't even know what was inside of it. I just hid it in the attic until I was able to return it to him and…."

While she is talking her husband walks out of the courtroom.

Dina stands up and screams. "Tony, Tony please I am so sorry."

Her attorney stands and intercepts, "Judge in light of this new information can I please request a recess I need to consult with my client."

The judge allows a recess.

Dina and her attorney are escorted in a quaint room to discuss what just transpired.

Dina's attorney is understandably pissed.

Tony storms in. He is raging with anger. "What the hell is going on Dina? You met someone? All this time you have been lying to my face."

Dina's attorney leaves the couple alone.

Tony is standing at a distance waiting for his wife to explain herself.

Dina cries out to her husband trying to explain that the night wasn't planned.

Tony with a poker face says, "Is that supposed to make me feel better? I can't do this. I have tried over and over to communicate with you and you just keep lying to me!"

Dina, knowing she should have not allowed this to go on for so long finally comes clean to her husband. "Tony please forgive me I know I was wrong I felt it in my spirit but I don't know, it happened and everything kept happening so fast but I need you right now. I didn't commit any crime! It just doesn't make sense."

Tony takes off his wedding ring, hurls it towards his wife and storms out of the room.

Dina is crying hysterically.

A few moments later Dina is back in the courtroom. She is instructed to return to the stand.

The state's attorney immediately rebegins. "Dina, let me remind you that you are still under oath. Prior to the recess you stated for the first time since you were charged that you met up with a man and he in fact is the owner of the black bag, Tell the court who the man is please."

Dina informs the court she doesn't know who the man is as she never verified his name or identity.

Everyone in the courtroom is shocked and speechless.

The state's attorney now knows he has leverage. "So, let me get this right. You met a man and allowed him to go inside your hotel room. He just so happened to have a black bag that he somehow forgot in your room. You brought the bag home, yet you never opened the bag to see what was in it, then somehow the bag disappears...?!?!.......your honor I have no further questions."

The court rests.

The jury deliberates under sixty minutes before rendering a verdict.

Court is back in session the following day.

A juror stands up. "We the jury, in the case of armed robbery and 2nd degree murder find Dina Jackson *GUILTY* of all charges."

The judge is ready to render a sentence the same day. "In light of the verdict and the nature of the crimes, Dina you are sentenced to life in prison; this court is adjourned."

Kylie, who has been supportive of her friend Dina the entire time, runs out of the courtroom crying with Brittany following right behind her.

Dina collapses in the courtroom.

Dina is hauled off to prison. Within a few days of being speechless, she is sitting in a prison cell going through mail. She opens mail from her husband. It is a letter written in crayon from her son. Dina starts crying out very loudly and is approached by a guard.

Dina screams, *"I NEED TO GET OUT OF HERE NOW."*

The guard takes a deep breath. "Listen, I can't say that I know what you are feeling but I can tell you that it only gets easier if you accept your present situation while fighting for justice for yourself."

Days turn to weeks and weeks to months. Before long an entire year has passed by.

Dina is journaling in her cell when a guard informs her that she has a visitor; the visitor is her attorney.

Her attorney informs her he has an update. "Well, though I would love to let you walk out, actually it is more complicated than just letting that happen; but we appealed your case. Because there was no evidence tying you to the murder the judge dropped those charges. But there is still the question of the robbery and the fact that jewelry matching from the jewelry store was found inside your home. I wish you would have been honest at the beginning of this case Dina but the fact that you lied only made things worse. You were found guilty of the robbery in the first trial and there is not enough evidence to prove otherwise. Being that this is your first offense and the murder charge was dropped the judge still sentenced you to four years for the robbery. You have already served one year and the judge is aware of no incidents so I tried to get you out early but the judge didn't agree. He did however agree with you getting released into a mental institution because of your unstableness during this process. Listen, all you need to complete is half the time; one and a half years and then we can go before the judge and I am confident he will release you early. I know it doesn't sound fair but Dina no one ever found the black bag that you claimed to have in your attic. Your husband even informed the police during the hearing that your luggage was green. There was no black bag anywhere in the room when he went to get you and well, the judge, and everyone else is a bit concerned with your mental status especially knowing you called the police to report a bag that was never recovered. Eighteen more months Dina, I have the paperwork here. If you are in agreement then we can work on transferring you and before you know it you will be back home with your family. That is, of course, if it's what you want? This is your life and ultimately your decision."

Dina is still stuck on her attorney mentioning family. "Family? What family? Tony filed for divorce and my son doesn't even really know me anymore. *WHY DID I LIE.* I lost everything for what? All for one night that I regret."

Dina, though not happy with her outcome, does agree that being confined to a mental facility is more lenient than remaining in maximum security prison.

Within a few weeks, she is transferred to a facility sixty miles further east. Though Tony does not keep in contact with Dina directly, he does send photos and cards from their son.

Sitting at a table alone tapping her fingers on the table rocking back and forth one day, the nurse enters the room where Dina is confined to and informs her of her first visitor.

The nurse leaves the room. Dina is nervously waiting. As the door opens, she starts to smile from ear to ear in anticipation of it being her husband or friends, but her facial expression quickly changes to horror when she sees who it is.

Karen walks in the room.

Dina now has a look that could kill. "What are you doing here?"

Karen smiles. "Well Dina I am a woman of my word. During the meeting at work, when you were employed by me, I informed the team that everyone affiliated with meeting goals would be getting a bonus and I would deliver it personally. I am late, I know, but there was no way I was visiting that God-awful prison you were housed."

Dina, with mixed emotions says, *"What did you do! You are the reason I have been going through hell what did you do?"*

Karen sarcastically says, "I don't have to take this from some ex-con, I came here to give you your bonus, now here, try not to spend it all in one place."

Karen slides an envelope on the table towards Dina.

"I am sorry." Dina cries. "Please sit down. I am just frustrated and I need closure I just don't understand how it is that you knew of the black bag, that day at your office, you specifically said a black bag. No one else knew about the bag. Please just tell me how *you* knew."

Karen looks at Dina. "Like I said, I only came to drop off your bonus I really can't...."

Before she could finish Dina interrupts. "I need rest. I have not rested for over a year. Please, talk to me."

Karen ponders her thoughts for a moment. "It is not what I know, it's who I know. Steve is my former lover."

Dina is not understanding. "I don't follow, Steve? Who is that is he involved some way, Steve? I don't know anyone by that name."

Karen is now clapping. "Wow, you know Dina you should really be careful about guys you allow in your hotel room."

Dina's eyes are wide open.

Karen has an evil look in her eyes. "Now, as I said, Steve, well he was my weakness for a long time, you know the 'forbitten fruit' for a married woman. Gorgeous isn't he."

Dina stands up on her feet in shock. "Oh my God. I can't breathe, help me, oh God I need a minute to take it all in." Dina takes a few moments to gather her thoughts. She is light-headed and needs to take a seat. It is all becoming clear. All of the pieces to the puzzle are aligning. "So, I was right you did set me up, you only hired me to help him get his black bag. Oh my God and I was so stupid I gave him my business card that night at the hotel. It had my email address on it, that's how you knew how to reach out to me, then you offered me a job and I took the bait. Once I was hired you had my address and phone number and oh my God you knew my every move. You had me work late hours so that he could try to come in my home and get the bag but when that didn't work you, oh my God, the free hotel stay?!? That was all part of your plan wasn't it. I didn't win the free hotel, did I? That was all a part of your plan to lure me away from home so that your lover could get the bag because you knew neither me nor my husband would be home. He knew where the bag was. I told him when he came by unannounced that night that it was in the attic so all he needed was a way inside when my family and I were not home and oh my God I fell for it all, the job, the getaway, me telling you and the team about how I was going to purchase a potted plant. He placed a piece of the jewelry stolen in the plant to frame me once he got the bag and then you anonymously called the police. Your lover robbed the jewelry store and killed Kylie's dad. *Your lover killed my best friends' dad*! I was just a pawn in his scheme. He was the one that witness saw running. He ran straight to my hotel room and later when he left the next morning, the police spotted him walking from the hotel and they suspected he was involved in the crime because he was in the area wearing all black and they picked him up. Then he called you and he gave you my business card information and you handled the rest. Your lover was released from jail shortly after because of lack of evidence because *I HAD THE EVIDENCE!!!* The whole time I had the evidence in my attic and never even knew."

"Bravo," smirks Karen. "You are clever for a black woman. My business was drowning after bad investments so one night I called my secret and forbitten chocolate flame and ironically, he was having some financial difficulties of his own. Luckily only an old black man died. Initially no one was supposed to get hurt. Just a quick robbery and a few millions in my business account so that I could meet my financial goals for the year and put some quick cash in Steve's pockets. But things didn't quite work out that way……well, you wanted closure Dina, there you have it. Glad I could be of service to you."

Karen proceeds to leave then turns around and looks Dina straight in the eyes and says, "You may want to be more careful about who you spend your time with, you had it all and didn't realize it. *You people* always want to be greedy and are never satisfied. It's not good enough that you get to live in our neighborhoods, work in the same places as us, breathe our fine air, and shop in our stores. You feel the need to want more? Why? You will never be on the same level as we are; *NEVER*. We tolerate you and try our best to be cordial but you people are weird as fuck.

Luckily for you I was able to teach you that a night of pleasure can lead to a lifetime of regret. Learn to stay in your lane because you will never be welcome in mine."

Dina grabs a pen from the table and journals her thoughts….

Don't gamble unless you are prepared to lose. Was life really that bad? Were you ultimately not happy? You had it all, everything one could dream but that wasn't enough, you just had to resort to things obscene. Do you not know that the death of joy is to compare what you have, where you are, and what you want? But you don't comprehend, you act like you have no understanding. This isn't just your life it involves your family. A family that loves you, adores you, and wants you to have the best, but that wasn't good enough, you just had to have more to try and feel worthy like the rest. Stop letting people pump your head, stop thinking the grass is greener as you will soon discover that where you resided was so much cleaner.

We Woke Up

Women Lead

Thomas, a well know councilman addresses the public during a town hall meeting hosted by he and his wife Karen. "Welcome everyone. I am so glad you all were able to join my wife and I today. As you all know I have great love for the Bayou. I was born and raised right down the street from here, graduated from the state university, built my home from the ground up, and started my life in the place that I love; the bayou. I have been the voice of the people for over thirty years and I want to be the first to announce some amazing news that will bring about great change for this community. The town has approved the new budget proposal to hire a full time City President and I am proud to say that I have humbly accepted the position. I need you all to sign the petition going around and within thirty days I will officially become your City President."

Karen stands up with a petition and passes it around to be signed.

The crowd is shocked and somewhat confused. The petition goes around and people are signing it.

Sophia, a new resident of the city looks around and turns to Cindy and Thelma, two long term residents who are sitting beside her. "Ok I know I am new to this town and well this is my first meeting but um, did I miss something? What is going on? I am so confused right now."

Thelma is looking at her watch. "Child it is almost 4pm, my granddaughter will be home from the after-school program at any moment just sign the damn paper so we can all go home." Thelma signs the paper and passes it to Cindy.

Cindy signs the paper then says, "It doesn't pay to ask questions. Thomas always has and always will run this town. He is an egotistical pig who believes women belong in the kitchen and bedroom while white men run the country. He has been very vocal on his stance on women rights or the lack of rights women should have. The men respect him and the women cater to him in-spite of, so the sooner you accept it the better off you will be. Besides Thelma is right the after-school club will be dropping the kids home soon. My daughter does after school tutoring there, her grades have improved significantly. That program is such a blessing, so accept whatever Thomas is doing and move the petition along so we can all go home."

Sophia is now upset and somewhat shocked. "Accept it? But how? Why? Like what kind of place is this where you have a meeting, get folks to sign a form, then you are all of a sudden running the city? It just doesn't make sense to me. Where I am from…."

Sophia is cut off by Karen. "Where you are from is not important, it's where you are that matters. Word around town is that you are new to this community, and well you don't want to start off on the wrong foot in a new community, do you? I mean you want folks to like you and respect you. Now my husband is going to run this town with or without your John Handcock so I suggest you keep your unnecessary sarcastic remarks to a minimum."

Karen nearly steps on Sophia's toes as she walks away.

Thelma laughs out loud. "Child she really did tell you, didn't she? I have to go. My granddaughter will be home from school any minute now."

As Thelma is walking out, she overhears a conversation between Thomas and Karen.

Thomas is attempting to whisper but isn't doing a great job at it. "Oh, my goodness can you believe how quick this meeting was. That was easier than I thought it would be, I should have added that each member of the city would give me their first born, they probably would have still signed it not knowing what it read. Wow these folks are something else. In thirty days, I will officially be running this city and the first thing I plan to do is tear down that old building on Main street and turn it into my headquarters. Oh, I just can't wait. It will be amazing. I will have a full staff working for me, the city will foot the bill, and you my darling will be my personal little secretary."

Karen smirks as she says, "Cheers to us darling."

Thelma is now standing with her mouth wide open in shock. She turns around to go and tell the others what she just heard but as she is walking towards them her phone rings.

Thelma walks away and answers the phone.

Patricia, her granddaughter, is on the other line. She has returned home but forgot her key so she is waiting outside for her grandmother.

Thelma who is usually home by this time informs her granddaughter that she is on her way back home.

Thelma leaves. Everyone is starting to leave but Sophia is still sitting in awe of what took place.

Sophia wonders aloud. "Is this even legal? Just sign a paper and that's it. This doesn't make sense."

Thomas is walking near her.

 Sophia sees him. "Thomas, can I have a moment of your time?"

Thomas stops walking and turns facing Sophia. "Of course, um have we met before? You don't look familiar to me."

"I actually just moved here, I expanded my business and well it was only right to move here and grow it as much as I can. I believe that the people of this community can profit from my business and I am excited to be a member of this community." Says Sophia proudly.

Thomas thinks for a second. "So, you are a hair stylist?"

Sophia stands to her feet. "Excuse me, what kind of assumption is that? Just because I am a black woman does not mean all I can do is style hair. How dare you insinuate what I do." Sophia, now upset and offended, is standing with her arms crossed.

Thomas is standing as well. "My bad, my bad don't get your little panties in a knot you must be one of those sales reps. Look I am all for supporting. How much is your products? Better yet it doesn't matter. Put me down for two of whatever you are selling. I can get one for my wife and one for my girlfriend."

Sophia, now extremely furious, storms out of the room and doesn't even have the desire to talk with him.

Sophia is so upset that she is trembling. She attempts to locate the contact number of the woman that she was sitting by at the townhall meeting as she, Cindy, greeted Sophia at the beginning of the meeting by saying her full name. She is easy to be reached and located via social media. Thelma was then reached by Cindy; as the two are friends. Cindy and Thelma agree to go over to Sophia's house in a few days when they all have time, as they know that Sophia is furious from the townhall meeting.

After a few days pass the two ladies meet up at the home of Sophia.

Thelma is mesmerized by the home. "You have such a lovely home. I love how you decorated this place. You have class darling."

The three ladies laugh.

Sophia then stops laughing and says, "Thank you Thelma I am glad you like the house, but I sure didn't have class a few days ago at that meeting."

Cindy smiles. "You seemed fine to me. I mean you didn't sign the petition but that is nothing to be overly upset about."

Sophia respects that. "Thanks, but when you all left, I had a few words of exchange with Thomas."

Thelma is now intrigued. "Really? Oh my, what happened? Why didn't you call us sooner? Tell us all about it."

"Well," starts Sophia. "I simply wanted to know more about the petition and his new role in the city but before we could even talk about that he implied I was a hair stylist. Now don't get me wrong I respect all professions but why would he just assume what I do."

Thelma while looking at Sophia's hair says, "Well your hair is real pretty maybe he thought…."

Sophia interrupts. "No, he didn't think! He is so arrogant and believes that women are confined to certain professions. Does he not understand that we can be anything we want to be? There are millions of women who are doctors and lawyers, engineers and corporate business leaders. Why are folks so quick to just assume? It irritates me because I was raised that I am equal to the next person. Do men not understand that women can lead?"

Cindy is very excited. "Yes!! You are correct. We can do anything we want to. I have been wanting to go back to school to earn my degree to one day become an attorney and you know what, I think I will. You have motivated me to want to do better. I can lead the judicial system and one day possibly sit at the chair of the supreme court."

Thelma claps for the two ladies. "Well, alrighty then, now that we are done dreaming can we get back to reality, for just a minute."

Sophia looks at Thelma. "Thelma, the reality is that life is passing us by and we need to take life by the horns and fly."

Thelma smirks. "While y'all fly away I will be right here. Look I understand you all are younger than me and believe that you can do great things and who knows maybe y'all can but the fact is that down in the bayou we have limited options. And with Thomas running the city those choices are going to get even smaller. Do y'all know that he is planning to tear down that old building on Main street? He wants to make a headquarter for his office there. Why does he need all that space? I mean it just doesn't make sense to spend the city's money on a building for him when there are so many other things that need to be done here."

Sophia is not happy with what Thelma said. "Tear down a building? Really? For his own personal headquarters that is a bit much, who in the world would agree to that. I mean the tax payers have a right to fight him on that. He may be the new head man in charge soon but to tear down a building well I vote no!"

Thelma's telephone rings.

Thelma answers. "Hello, why yes this is she. What!!!! Are you serious? What happened? How? Oh my, I am on my way."

Cindy and Sophia yell. "What's wrong?"

Thelma is in a panic. "That was the school calling. Patricia has just been suspended for fighting."

Thelma is noticeably upset. "I just don't know what to do with her. I took my granddaughter Patricia in after she was giving her parents trouble. It was a little rocky at first but once I enrolled her in the after-school club, I started to see a change for the better. She made new friends and even picked up her grades in school through after school tutoring. I just don't know what happened to make her fight another student. But I tell you what I am going to find out. I will talk with you ladies later, I got to go."

Just as Thelma opens the door to leave Patricia is standing in the door way.

Patricia greets Thelma.

Thelma is now irritated. "Let me guess, you forgot your key again and tracked me down on that cellular device?! I swear Patricia you would lose your head if it wasn't attached to your body and what the heck happened at school today and don't you dare lie to me because your principal already contacted me. What is going on?" She pauses. "Well speak! I am waiting!"

Patricia looks big eyed at her grandmother. "So, there is this boy and well Tosha said that Jenny said that I told Rebecca that Colby said that…."

Thelma has her hands on her hips. "What in the foolery are you saying child? Why were you fighting?"

Patricia says, "Granny I am trying to tell you."

"Well give me the straight to the point version. I am old, I don't have all day for this nonsense." Says Thelma as she is getting annoyed.

Patricia is now breathing hard as her grandmother cut her off while she was trying to tell her what happened a few short minutes ago. "A boy told me that a girl told him I liked him, so I found the girl and beat her up!"

Thelma looking at her granddaughter in confusion. "What boy? Do you like him?"

Patricia is blushing. "Yes, but that wasn't her place to tell him and now I am suspended from school and I can't go to the after-school club tomorrow because they follow the same system as the school."

Thelma is shaking her head. "You know I don't want you fighting. You are doing so good here. One of the reasons your parents allowed you to live with me was to get you back on track. But I can't and won't keep you here if you are not going to follow the rules. You can't go around fighting because you get upset. You know better. Now soon as we get home you can hand me your cell phone and laptop. You are on punishment for two weeks."

"Two weeks? With no phone? Granny that is not fair. It wasn't even my fault." Says Patricia almost in tears.

Thelma is tapping her left foot in anger. "Well, did you fight at school today?'

Patricia is now irritated. "Yes but…."

Thelma interrupts. "But nothing. Now no more excuses or I will extend your punishment an additional week. Fighting at school behind some boy. Child it doesn't make no darn sense. Now tell these ladies good-bye it's time to go home."

As the ladies are saying good-bye Sophia gets an alert on her phone. "Oh my goodness. Thomas has called an emergency townhall meeting for tomorrow."

Cindy is shocked as they just had a townhall meeting a few days ago. "Really? Why?"

Sophia, while looking at her phone says, "I'm not sure. It doesn't say the reason. I signed up to get text alerts of meetings in the city when I first moved here. You know to network and grow my business. Do you all think it has anything to do with his upcoming new position?"

Thelma chuckles. "Don't know but I will be there. I owe it to the neighborhood to stay informed so that I can tell everyone what I know and I need up to date information."

Cindy agrees with attending as well. "I will be there too. I wonder what's going on now."

The ladies don't see or speak again until the next day at the town hall meeting, which they all attend.

Thelma is looking at her watch. "I know this meeting better not last long because I am tired. You know I stayed up all night watching the house around the corner from me. They were having a party and didn't even think to invite me."

Cindy and Sophia laugh.

Patricia who is at the meeting with her grandmother does not want to be there and complains of boredom.

Thelma looks at her granddaughter and snaps at her. "I would rather you be at the after-school club but you can't go there because you were suspended. Now sit down quietly!"

Thomas and his wife Karen walk in. With them is an unknown man. Karen and the unknown man sit down as her husband walks to the podium to address everyone.

Thomas addresses the crowd of citizens. "Hello everyone and thank you for coming under such short notice. I know that you all have busy schedules so I will try my best to be short and to the point. As you all know a few days ago, well let's insinuate, almost 30 days ago you all voted for me to be the next City

President and well by law I have to stand before you prior to my term going into effect and let you know of my plans for the future. Since there were no opponents naturally, I will automatically be sworn in by the district judge and I will begin my term soon.

Everyone is looking around the room confused. Sophia stands up and without the power to speak says, "Sorry to interrupt but when did everyone vote? I get alerts on my phone and I never received any voting information."

Cindy chimes in. "Neither did I, what's going on Thomas?"

Thomas calmly states, "How soon you all forget what we discussed at the last meeting. We discussed me being the next City President."

Sophia, who is still standing says, "Actually you discussed it while everyone just listened."

Everyone in the crowd agrees.

Thomas is now getting agitated. "First off chick, sit down. Now as I was stating you all voted. Karen, make yourself useful and bring me my folder dear."

Karen gets up and hands Thomas a folder. He takes out the signed petition from the first meeting.

Thomas continues talking. "Do you all know what this is? This is your votes."

Sophia with her hands up says, "No it's not *that* is a petition that you *made* us sign."

Thomas looks and says, "Made you sign? We are all adults here no one made you sign anything. You all willingly signed this. Kelvin can you come up and read this to everyone and explain the process please."

Kelvin is the unknown man that entered the room with Thomas and his wife.

Kelvin gets up and addresses the crowd. Thomas is standing beside him.

"Good evening everyone my name is Kelvin Ford. I am the Chief Advisor to the Governor's office. According to the city ordinance I have to be present prior to any swearing in of new officers of the city to ensure that all policies and procedures have taken place. Now this is the form you all signed. It states:

'Thomas will be the new City President. He will be a voice for the people. He will be allowed to make decisions as needed. The city will only have one townhall meeting a year and it will be a review of everything that Thomas has decided to do solely based on his decisions. The city and all citizens agree to give Thomas the full annual city recreational budget of

$450,000.00. Per city law any expenses over $250,000 at one time must be approved by the town. By signing below the citizens of the town agree to the following terms:

- *Thomas has full rights and responsibility of the town.*
- *The town will only have one annual meeting.*
- *Thomas will take $2,500,000.00 from the annual budget, tear down the old building on the corner of Main street, and make it his headquarters. He has the right to take the remaining budget and hire a team of consultants and city advisors.*
- *Thomas will only have to consult with his immediate team. The citizens will have no voice.'*

This was signed by over 95% of the town. In fact, most of you appear to be present today." Kelvin then looks around into the crowd.

Everyone is speechless and confused.

Kelvin resumes speaking, "Now according to the ordinance prior to the swearing in I have to verify that these signatures are legit and that no one else is running for city president, then we can officially place Mr. Thomas in office. The swearing in for the next city officers is less than a week away so you all can understand why there is such a need to have this urgent meeting tonight. All right, well if there is no other business and all of you can say *'I'* to the agreement of what was just spoken in regards to Thomas being the new City President then this meeting can be adjourned.

Do you the citizens of the town agree that …….'

Sophia stands up and screams, *'I OBJECT.'*

Kelvin and everyone are in awe.

Thomas leans over to Kelvin. "She was one of the 5% that didn't vote for me."

Kelvin looks at Sophia. "Ma'am please have a seat. The people have spoken."

Sophia interjects. "No, the people have not. The people have been fooled and tricked! No one was explained all of these changes. We were told to sign and we did with no information. I mean seriously we didn't even get a chance to review anything he simply passed a paper stating it was some petition and we all signed and went home. This is an outrage and I have a good mind to call the news and report this whole foolishness."

Kelvin is now trying to take control of the meeting before it gets out of hand. "Wait ma'am. There is no need to get beside ourselves. Thomas, what is going on here? You told me everything was on the up and up. I mean seriously what is going on?"

Thomas, looking embarrassed yet cocky says, "These citizens agreed and now they are going back on their word. Look I am trying to bring about change. Take that old building on the corner of Main street, it's old and needs to be torn down. Instead of folks having to look at that they can look at my headquarters, come in and get valuable information about this great city. Besides having to drive past that building and see all those teenagers hanging around after school is a disgrace."

Patricia, who has been very quiet speaks up. "Wait are you trying to tear down the after-school club?"

Thelma to Patricia, "No dear hush up, the after-school club is on King street not Main street."

Kelvin corrects Thelma. "Well actually ma'am the actual mailing/city address for the after-school club is 9834 Main street, even though it's a corner lot, it's technically on Main street."

Thelma is outraged. "*YOU MEAN TO TELL ME YOU ALL ARE TRYING TO TAKE AWAY THE ONLY PLACE THESE KIDS HAVE! THEY GO THERE AFTER SCHOOL NOT TO HANG AROUND BUT TO GET TUTORING, COUNSELING, MENTORSHIP, PLAY FUN GAMES, STAY ACTIVE, AND MEET FRIENDS THEIR OWN AGE.*" Thelma calms herself down. "It gives them an option from being stuck in the house with the internet or worse in the street. There is absolutely no way that you can tear that place down! You just can't!"

Everyone is standing and arguing at this point.

Kelvin attempts to quiet the crowd of citizens. "Settle down everyone, settle down! I need everyone to sit down so that we can talk like rational adults. Now clearly there has been one or two steps that have been missed. According to the by-laws the majority votes will win in all elections. Now seeing that there is no other person running against Thomas regardless of steps that have been missed per the by-laws, he would still be the only running candidate. Now of course he will need training on the rules and by-laws in the future, seeing this meeting is a complete disaster, but because he is the only candidate, he will still be the new City President."

Sophia looks around. "I want to put my name in the ballot."

Everyone is looking in awe.

Thomas in an angry tone yells, "That is absorb. The election is a few days away. I mean even if you wanted to run against me you would not have time." Thomas starts laughing. "Crazy ass woman, I tell you just crazy."

Cindy stands up. "I second that nomination. I believe Sophia would do a great job."

Kelvin, with a grin, "Well, looks like we have a race on our hands."

Thomas is now standing with his hands bolted together. "There is no way. The election is merely a few days away."

Kelvin looks through his papers. "The election is six days away to be exact and per the by-law's anyone can enter the race prior to the election as long as they are a law-abiding citizen of the town for over thirty days."

Thomas smiles. "Well, there you have it. Race over. Sophia just moved here."

Kelvin to Sophia, "Is that true?"

Sophia says, "Well technically yes but I have been in business here for well over six months and my business is thriving."

Kelvin says, "I am sorry but unless you can prove that you have had residence here for over thirty days you can't legally run for office in this town."

Thomas now smiling from ear to ear says, "Well, that's that. I will see you all in less than a week at the polls. Oh, and Sophia since you want to be seen and heard so bad, you can bring the donuts and coffee on the day of election. *If* you do that well then maybe I can allow you a place on my team as my shoe shiner."

Patricia looks at Thelma. "Granny do something. He is going to tear down the after-school club. Please granny don't let him do that. Please it is all that I have."

Thomas overhears the conversation with Patricia and her grandmother. "Young lady if the after-school club is so important to you why are you here and not there?"

Patricia looks at him with a sassy stare. "Because I was suspended from school and over there. But what you are doing is wrong."

Thomas with a smirk, "Really? This coming from a delinquent juvenile."

Thelma stands to her feet. "Now you wait one damn minute Thomas you will not pre-judge my granddaughter. You are out of line."

Thomas who has known Thelma for years says, "Ms. Thelma now you know that I respect you. You are one of the elders of this community but she needs to stay in a child's place. She will find somewhere else to go. Oh, but make sure that it's not around my city because I will have you all arrested as I see fit."

Thelma is now beyond angry. "That's it I have had enough."

Cindy attempts to console her friend.

Thelma is almost in tears. "No, it is not okay. I will not calm down. I have lived in this city all my life. I have worked sometimes two jobs to make it. I have followed all of the rules of the land and went out of my way to help people. I will not allow anyone regardless of who they are to pre-judge me or my family. I have had enough!" Thelma is now screaming. *"KELVIN, HAS ANYONE SEEN KELVIN?"*

Kelvin who was sitting nearby speaking with citizens hears his name being called. "Here I am, is there something I can do for you?"

Thelma looks him directly in the eyes. "Yes, there is. There is a qualified, well rounded, caring person who wants to run against Thomas."

Kelvin trying to be understanding says, "Yes ma'am I understand your frustration but Sophia can't run, maybe next term though."

Thelma says to Kelvin, "I am not talking about Sophia. I want my name in the ballot."

Everyone stops and is standing with their mouth open.

Kelvin calls the city secretary to inform her that there is another possible candidate. Thelma is given information on how to follow the proper guidelines and be named on the ballot.

Shortly after everyone leaves the meeting site. That meeting is the talk of the town. Every store, restaurant, salon, gas station, the entire town is in awe of what transpired.

A few days go by.

Thelma is at home sitting alone in a room flipping through the pages of a book when Patricia walks into the room. "Hi granny what are you doing?"

Thelma looks at her granddaughter and says, "Just looking through this book. When I was only a little girl, I was given this very book about women who lead. Feminist leaders helped start some of the biggest organizations for women's rights. Addressing the depression and unhappiness of women forced by society into the role of a home maker or mother.

Patricia is in awe. "Wow women did awesome work and seemed to possibly have led the way for many women across America. Wait you still have that book after all this time?"

Thelma smiles. "Yes dear, because this book showed me time after time that I am enough. Regardless of how hard times get or how discouraged I may feel I read this book and I get inspired." Shortly after, Thelma puts her head down.

Patricia inquires of her grandmother's depressed look on her face.

Thelma, takes a deep breath. "I just wonder if I made the right decision. Look at me, I am not a spring chicken. I am an old lady, born from a line of slaves. I'm years past retirement age running against a man in the prime of his life for an office that I know little to nothing about. I just don't know; I don't know what the future will hold and it scares me. I have been thinking and I think that it may be best for me to just drop out of the race. I mean I am merely a woman; I should just accept the defeat that I know will come on the day of election. I am just too old and too tired to fight this fight."

Thelma sits in silence with her granddaughter for a few moments.

Patricia looks at Thelma. "Granny you are the strongest woman I know. Do you know why my parents sent me here? They did it because they knew that you would help shape me into the young woman that I need to be and you know what? They made a wise decision. You are amazing. I know I don't say it much and I can be a handful at times but you are the woman that I admire. You have worked hard, raised a beautiful family, built this great home, and you have become a leader to this community in more ways than one."

Thelma slightly picks up her head as Patricia keeps talking.

"Granny if you don't want to be the next leader because of a personal choice everyone will have to accept it because this has to be a personal decision. But I am telling you that you were born to lead. You are a true leader and I admire you. My only regret is that I am not old enough to vote because I would vote you in office tonight."

Thelma is chuckling. "Oh Patricia, I love you so much my dear."

Patricia kisses her grandmother on the cheek. "I love you too granny and I will do anything I can to help make your load a little lighter. I want to see you win."

Patricia and Thelma embrace with a warm hug before Patricia leaves the room.

Thelma stands and walks toward a mirror near her. She looks at her own reflection. "My name is Thelma and I want to be the next leader of this city. I want to make a difference." Thelma shrugs her shoulders. "No, that didn't come out right. Maybe I should start with a joke or tell a story. Oh my, what have I done. I only wanted to make a difference. I didn't like how Thomas was speaking and I ran off at the mouth. I don't have the education to lead a town, what am I going to do. My phone has been ringing off the hook these last few days. I can't eat or sleep I am all worried over what will happen. On the other hand, at least I tried right? I gave it my all. Oh boy were we busy this week. We marched all over the city with voting signs. I have shaken the hands of everyone in my path. I was interviewed by the news oh but this is all too much. And it all balls down to tonight. Tonight, is the last debate and the night where everyone votes. Oh, I am just a wreck. I am too old for this. What is wrong with me thinking I can lead. Lord I wish that Sophia could have ran, she would be awesome. She and Cindy have been such an amazing support system for me, they are just incredible women. Oh well, let me get dressed and ready for tonight." She takes deep breath. "Relax Thelma, relax."

The time everyone has been waiting for arrives.

Patricia, Cindy, Sophia, and Karen are all sitting down in the crowd of people. Thelma and Thomas are on the front row sitting on opposite sides of one another and Kelvin is near the podium.

Kelvin walks to the podium and addresses everyone. "Welcome fellow citizens. It was busy the last few days, but the time is winding down. Tonight, we will hear from our candidates and take questions.

Thankfully for technology we will be able to see who the winner is tonight. You see we have voting polls here and everyone at home, those who could not physically be here, they are watching from home and they were each given a secure voting ID password to call in and cast their vote. Within minutes of the votes being accounted for we will have a new projected leader of this town. Right now, I need both candidates to come to the podium please. You each will have one minute to tell the people why you feel you should be the next leader. Each of you will then answer questions from the audience then we will make final remarks and we will cast our votes. Thelma let's start with you."

Thelma is very nervous at first. "Well as you all know I have lived in this community for many years. I have seen both good and bad leadership but what I have yet to see is fair leadership. I want to be fair. I want to listen to the people and be a voice when there is none. So many people have great ideas and we need to listen to them. I want to be able to show the community that we care. I want to help the youth grow up knowing that this community has always been there for them and always will be. I want to keep the after-school program open and bring more positivity to this great city. I know that I can do it but not alone. I need the help of you. I need the help of this community."

Everyone claps and shouts in agreement.

Kelvin then turns to Thomas and allows him to address everyone.

Thomas with no nervous looks about him boldly says, "I have been in leadership of this city for practically all of my adult life. Prior to this position even coming around I was here. I have been here and I will always be here. It is time that my past years of service be put to good use and I officially be given the title I deserve. We need new businesses and information centers. I have already reached out to a major construction firm out of Georgia to come and tear down that old after-school building and start my headquarters. We will see a great change and we will move forward."

A few people clap. Karen stands up and applauds loudly.

Kelvin who is remaining bias and has not applauded any candidate continues to moderate the debate. "Alright that was well said from both parties. Now do we have a few questions from the citizens?"

Sophia raises her hand and is called on to ask her question. "Yes, my question is for Thomas. What do you propose will happen to the youth once you tear down the building?"

Thomas responds. "Well, I suppose they will go home and spend quality time with their families. Look I know a lot of you are upset about the building being torn down but I have contacted the best construction firm in the business, some of you have heard of them they are called DT constructions and they are huge. Bringing them here to build my headquarters may lead to them building other businesses and because of the money we are spending on my headquarters who knows they may come in and offer to do more work for us at a discount price. It is a win for everyone."

Everyone claps. Karen yells, "New beginnings for all."

Thelma starts to walk away from where she was standing.

Kelvin notices and addresses her in front of everyone. "Thelma, we aren't finished. We still have time for a few more questions."

Thelma is looking highly disappointed. "What's the use? Thomas has called in a big shot company and I can't compete with that. I love this community I genuinely do, but I just can't compete."

Sophia stands up and speaks out of turn. "Thelma please don't quit I will help you. My business gives back all the time. I would be honored to help you any way I am able. But please don't quit you have come too far to turn around now."

Kelvin leans over to Thomas asking, "Business? What business does she have?"

Thomas leans closer to Kelvin and says, "She owns some little hairstyling type of woman's company."

Sophia hears Thomas and with a very loud voice says, *'NO I don't Thomas. I own DT constructions.'*

Everyone gasps.

Thelma is at a stand-still. "Wait I am confused. You have been helping Thomas? When did you all talk about this? Please somebody tell me what is going on?"

Thomas is looking just as confused as everyone else. "No this can't be, I mean you can't be the owner. I called the corporate office in Georgia. I spoke to the man there. He said he was the Chief Operating Officer of the company. I told him all about my plans and my project and he said he would talk with his business partner and get back with me. I have his contact in my phone there is no way you own DT constructions; they are the biggest construction company in the South."

Sophia is now grinning happily. "If you spoke to the COO then you spoke with my husband. He is *my* business partner. DT constructions was named in honor of my late dad (Douglas Thompson) I started the business after graduating with my MBA. Shortly after I started the business my husband worked as a part time construction worker to fully learn the business so that he could come aboard as my partner. My husband and I haven't talked much about the Georgia business and new opportunities because we have been so busy talking about everything going on here with the growth of this location. I am the CEO of the business. He stayed back to help run the Georgia office while I came here to purchase our home and get things settled. He will be moving here soon as I recently closed on our new home, the one I recently bought us. Oh, and Thomas, we will not be going into business with you. Instead, I would like to publicly endorse Thelma and assist with her vision of leading this community. That is if she doesn't give up and quit the race."

Patricia who has heard everything walks over to Thelma. "Granny please don't give up the community needs you; I need you. Just think if other women would have given up? What if they didn't help start national women's organizations, where would you be? I started reading, '*Take off the Mask,*' by a female writer and it helped me to find my voice and be who I was created to be, please granny *FIND* your voice and be heard."

Thelma puts her right arm around her granddaughter then looks to Kelvin and says, "Forgive me for attempting to step down in the middle of questioning please proceed."

Kelvin addresses the crowd. "Do we have any more questions for the two candidates?"

Kelvin looks around. "Well, if no one has anything else to say we will have final remarks from the two candidates. Thomas you may speak first. What is one comment that you want everyone in this room to remember?"

Thomas looks out at everyone and says, "I am for the future, vote for me and you will see change."

Kelvin looks at Thelma and gives her permission to speak.

Thelma looks at the crowd and in a firm strong voice she says, "Women lead from the front. We are a force to be reckoned with."

Everyone claps for both candidates.
Kelvin directs everyone to the voting area.
Everyone gets up and forms a line. Citizens quietly begin to vote.

Karen is pacing back and forth; Thomas walks up to her.

Thomas looks at his wife and asks, "Karen, what's wrong why aren't you in line to vote?"

Karen with tears in her eyes says, "I didn't realize that people can vote from their home. Do you know that means we may lose? I only rigged the voting machines. Now what? We can't let *her* win. Can you imagine what would happened if *they* had control? This city would go downhill and be worth nothing."

Thomas is now upset. "You are my wife, get your shit together bitch. Get on the phone and call people; *make* them vote for me."

Karen is hesitant.

Thomas looks at his wife, grabs her by the neck and says, "Look, I don't have time for this bullshit; all women are worthless. I need to go win over more votes."

Karen is unsure making phone calls will even work but she picks up her phone and walks away as she is committed to doing whatever her husband instructs her to do.

Within a few hours everyone is finished voting and sitting down with anticipation.

Kelvin, from the podium with an envelope in hand, proceeds to address everyone. "Thank you to both candidates. Can we give them both a round of applause? They ran clean races. I must say that this election was like none this community has ever seen. This election had the highest turn out in history. People who never voted in this town came out and voted. History was truly made tonight in terms of voting. We must remember that all votes count. Every election matters. We must always use our voice beyond arguments and strife and remember that voting is our weapon. That alone unlocks the key to the future. No one knows what the next day holds but with the correct politicians in office there is hope for better days. Well, let me not keep you all any longer. Thank goodness for technology because we already have the votes counted. In this envelope are the results. My hands are shaking, this has been one of the most memorable elections I have ever been part of and I must say it has been quite the experience."

 Kelvin takes a deep breath, then opens the envelope. "Here goes."

There is a pause. No one is talking. No one is on their cell phone. Everyone in the room is staring at Kelvin, waiting impatiently.

"And the new leader of this great city is:"

THELMA HOPKINS

After a few moments of allowing everyone to congratulate the new City President, Kelvin, addresses the crowd for one final time. "Thelma has made history tonight. No woman has ever held this position. Thelma is the first woman to ever be voted into any position in this city. Thelma you made history; may you please come up and address your townspeople."

Thelma, while in tears, walks up to the podium to address the crowd of voters. She looks around, over 75 percent of the voters are women. Thelma looks and sees her granddaughter and smiles. "We are the women of America and we lead. Millions of American women are leaders. We are not confined to the domestic role nor do we have to settle for less. We can start our own business, hire our own teams, and run our own country. I dare you to find your voice in this world. A female should not expect leniency, but neither should she be frowned upon by men. A girl who dreams becomes a woman who leads. I am a woman. I stand tall. I am a leader and I have made history as your first female City President. But we must not stop here. We must start by removing the wrong elected officials and start hiring and voting for those who genuinely care for the entire human race. We must not define a person by their mistakes or judge based off the opinions of others. We must contact local government and fight against injustice. We the people must be the change we desperately seek and lead this land."

Thomas stands up, roughly grabs Karen by the wrist, and the two abruptly walk out of the building without uttering a word.

Thelma returns home and journals her thoughts….

Leaders Lead. Everyone is a leader until it's time to lead. We hide behind cameras, text messages and social media. We talk good game and are very quick to point blame, but when the opportunity arises what do we do?

You can't lead when it's convenient nor should you run and hide. When you confessed to being a leader there were certain laws that you were instructed to abide.

Leaders are needed.

They are far and few. But if no one comes forward, what do we do?

We Woke Up.

The outcome of a worldwide awakening.

Petitions started, riots sparked, old cases were reviewed and reopened. People demanded answers. Police seemingly were held accountable, stricter policies were implemented in place, and America slowly began to wake up.

People who did not understand the 'why' became defensive, while others became educated.
Lifelong friends turned to enemies and the world slowly divided. Racism was evident
And for what, because of a single event?

No, not because of one event but due to every wrongdoing ever committed. For every single job offer denied simply because of the color of skin. For every home loan being denied, for every time a black person was told no simply because of the color of their skin. The nations' outcry was not simply because of a few circumstances, but instead, a result of years when people felt they lived in a world where they did not have the complexion for protection.

For every time someone 'fit the description' because pants hung too low, for every traffic stop that led to an unlawful arrest. The outcry was for every job applicant that met the qualifications on paper but didn't meet the skin tone in person. For every little girl told 'you're pretty for a black girl' for every young boy told 'pick up a ball and shut up.' This was for the man who was guilty before his trial started, for every family member who had to be educated on what not to say or do because it could be held against them. This was not because of one person but for all persons. This was for people who were never trying to be better than another race but instead stand alongside all races with dignity and pride.

We woke up now what?

This is not 'just another movement'. Instead, we as Americans have to find a way to forgive hurt from the past but never forget. We must remember that those of us living were never slaves nor were any of our fellow neighbors slave owners. We must never forget our history but instead allow it to be a reminder of how far we've come and allow the journey to become the foundation of where we are aiming to reach. We must choose to heal effectively to break chains of yesterday and embrace what lies ahead. The world is awake; lawmakers are listening, corporations are seemingly understanding. And though nothing can bring back those that were lost along the way; nothing can change the pain endured. We can be sure that we never allow America to go back to sleep. We must stand our ground and demand justice for all. We are fortunate to be educated enough to know that we were never trying to be better but we do deserve equality.

We Woke Up….
By: Lynfree J.

Lynfree J. is an American Writer. She writes books to jumpstart conversations needed around the world. From Racism and Injustice, to Mental Health and Christianity, **Lynfree J.** has tackled topics that aim to wake you up. Her books allow you to re-examine your mindset into understanding the concept that there is more to life than what the eyes may see.

'We climb hills in hopes of elevation that leads us to the other side where there is the unification of protection for every generation.'

-Lynfree J.

www.ingramcontent.com/pod-product-compliance
Lightning Source LLC
Chambersburg PA
CBHW021111110726
47900CB00007B/2134